"Lovely, lovely," he crooned in sincere admiration. The touch of his fingertips brushing up the outside of her thigh and sent a mellow warmth through Gloria, who swayed slightly, lightheaded with the pleasure of her lover's delicate, teasing caress. Using just the pads of his fingers, he glided along the gauzy nylon, following the ridge of the leg band of her panties through the snug press of her slick pantyhose. His fingers continued along the curving elastic band following it into the juncture between her thighs . . .

Also available from Blue Moon Books by Don Winslow

GLORIA'S INDISCRETION

DON WINSLOW

BLUE MOON BOOKS
NEW YORK

Gloria's Indiscretion

© 1993, 2004 by Don Winslow

Published by
Blue Moon Books
An Imprint of Avalon Publishing Group Incorporated
245 West 17th Street, 11th floor
New York, NY 10011-5300

First Blue Moon Books edition 2004

First published by Masquerade Books in 1993

ISBN 1-56201-430-7

9 8 7 6 5 4 3 2 1

Printed in Canada
Distributed by Publishers Group West

FOREWORD

The ties that bind us, one to another, are seldom neatly drawn. How can one map the complex bloodlines between mother and child, sister or brother, or even the most casual relationships when they must inevitably bear ghostly vestiges of those other more primal, more enduring bonds? How can one trace the twisted lines of intense, sometimes chaotic, often ambivalent feelings that comprise the intricate skein of human attachments?

And what of love? To try to unravel erotic entanglements is a task worthy of the psychoanalyst's attention, for it is only through the medium of that arcane art that the twisting labyrinth of the psyche can be adequately explored.

In *Gloria's Indiscretion* we are presented with a case study of sorts, an intense exploration of the tangled lifelines of three people drawn together in their obsessive pursuit of sensual pleasure.

—Don Winslow
Copenhagen

CHAPTER ONE

HE PARKED BEHIND a sleek green Jaguar, the last of a long curving line of convertibles, sports cars, and elegant sedans—the imported, expensive toys that lined the side of the sweeping gravel driveway. The sounds of the party could be heard coming from the pool behind the huge house, a sprawling structure of glass and steel that jutted out on pillars of poured concrete. The floodlit slabs loomed large and impressive against the nighttime sky. Decker headed toward the noise.

By now the party had developed a life of its own. Ali was nowhere to be seen, but things were humming along; the absence of a host didn't seem to matter one bit. Guests and various hangers-on were clustered in little knots, sprinkled about the pool and spilling through the sliding glass doors into the spacious, starkly modern interior.

From somewhere, a stereo pounded out a super-charging rock song. The angry music battled against the rising murmur of voices, and was sporadically drowned out by sudden bursts of laughter. And through the babble of voices, and the noise, and the din of the throbbing music, there ran a ripple of excitement, an underlying tension, that Decker inevitably associated with Ali's parties.

This was a place where the rich and powerful came to meet the young and beautiful. They were people on the make, drawn to Suleiman Ali as people had always been drawn to the classic middleman, the arranger of deals, the gloriously unabashed, unrepentant pimp.

Decker paused in the doorway, scanning the eager faces of well-tailored men and elegant women in their fashionable evening wear. His gaze passed over the crowd without much interest. There was no one he particularly wanted to talk to. He paused on the edge, then stepped down into the sunken living room, plunging into the crowd, making his way toward a corner bar where an overworked bartender was mixing and pouring endless rounds of drinks.

He felt better with a drink in his hand, prepared to let himself slowly drift to the periphery, slipping easily into his comfortable role of perpetual onlooker. He settled his long lean frame against the staircase that led up to the bed-rooms on the second floor, leaning back, letting his gray eyes take in the bubbling scene with casual indifference.

Suddenly, a stir in the corner of the room caught his attention. There was a ripple of laughter, and then, at the center of small knot of men, he saw her: a tall elegant brunette with large expressive eyes, and a thick mane of lustrous black hair that tumbled down in loose folds over her bare shoulders. A little black dress smoothed her fem-inine curves, while its scoop-necked front and thin spaghetti straps left her supple arms and gracefully con-toured neck and shoulders all deliciously exposed. It was her laughter that caused heads to turn, a deep full-throated laugh, low and earthy, punctuated by a quick toss of the head, that sent her thick hair shaking merrily. At her laughter, the men around her closed in, drawn by her infectious enthusiasm.

Bright and animated, the dark-haired girl resumed her story that the laughter had momentarily interrupted. With her drink cradled in one hand, she raised the other to weave expressive gestures in the air. Decker admired the graceful movement of that slender aristocratic hand, and the way she bestowed her easy smile on her captivated audience. He watched the devastating way she used her eyes: dark intelligent eyes, sparkling with childlike eagerness, flitting from one man to the next. And when those eyes found a man's, the object of her gaze would find himself unhinged by that look, a look that said that he, and he alone, was the only man in the world.

Decker was instantly intrigued. He found himself moving closer till he stood just outside of her little circle of admirers, watching her face: the finely chiseled features, and the rich folds of raven-black hair; the bare-shouldered glamour of that little dress. At that moment the girl happened to look up, and her eyes caught his watching her. The large dark eyes paused, seemed to consider his for a moment, then moved on. Decker felt the unmistakable twinge of excitement, a reflexive quickening of anticipation when their eyes met.

The contact had lasted the merest moment. Then she turned aside, leaning over toward one of her companions, an older dignified man with a thick mane of gray hair who looked like an aging movie star. She touched him lightly on the arm, and leaned close to say something in his ear. He beamed with pleasure, pleased to have her exclusive attention.

Wildly excited by the possibilities that her look seemed

to offer to him, Decker backed away, and looked about him, desperate for someone who could help. Anxiously, he searched the room and, as luck would have it, spotted his host descending the stairs, a smile of papal beneficence on his handsome Semitic face.

Ali was slightly high. His tie was gone, and his open shirt revealed several loops of gold chain entangled in the thick fur of his broad barrel chest. He steadied himself on the banister with his hairy left paw, while his right arm loosely encircled the narrow waist of a young blonde, whose sleek tanned body seemed barely contained in a tight white dress. As they came down the steps, listing slightly, Ali slipped his hand down to caress the rounded mounds of that skirted bottom, giving the girl a friendly squeeze through the thin dress. She giggled and snuggled up against him, delivering a quick kiss, and sending both of them tottering precariously on the bottom step.

Decker was already pushing his way toward his blissful host.

"Ali, I need to talk to you."

"Thomas!" The smile broadened widely on the dark craggy face. "Having a good time?"

Decker smiled, and opened his mouth to say something, but his amiable host, not actually expecting a reply, rambled on expansively.

"A nice group, don't you think?" he nodded approvingly. "By the way, do you know Susan?"

Decker turned his attention to the thin-faced blonde who stood in stocking feet, swaying on the final stair, leaning on her short, stocky lover. Her dull blue eyes gazed down on Decker; her lips widened in the smile of the pleasantly plastered. Disheveled, her lipstick smeared, hair mussed, and her tight dress slightly askew, the girl must have recently made some hasty repairs, obviously without much success. Her small plump breasts, precariously

– 4 –

tucked away, threatened to spill out of the plunging neckline as she leaned down to give Decker a big, crooked smile.

Decker nodded to her, and said, as politely as he could manage: "Would you excuse us for a moment?"

He grabbed Ali by the arm and guided him down the final step, steering him to one side.

"Listen Ali, I need to know who that girl is . . . *that* one . . . over there."

"Who . . . oh yes, I see. You mean Gloria. Gloria Brennan," he pronounced emphatically. "She *is* something, isn't she? A real babe! And smart too! Yes, beautiful, and witty and charming; a nice package, no? But"—and this with a woeful sigh—"you must be careful there. There's something not quite right about that girl."

For the next few minutes the genial Egyptian supplied the details to his avid interrogator. There were things Ali knew about Gloria Brennan, and things he didn't know. He knew, for example, that she was single; divorced; no children. Though still in her thirties she was already a partner in one of the city's best-known law firms; an ambitious, hard-driving workaholic; a career woman, for whom men were an afterthought, useful occasionally, if they could conveniently fit into her life, but otherwise not to be taken all that seriously.

What he did not know was that Gloria Brennan had grown up as an only child of rich parents, a love-starved little girl who, left to her own devices, could never please a cold demanding mother. Her mother, Cynthia Brennan, was a small town girl, a ravishing beauty who had married at an early age. A perfectionist, she was constantly critical of her daughter, finding fault with the way she dressed and talked and walked, so that the girl increasingly turned to her father for affection.

And there she got a very different welcome indeed.

John Brennan was a big man; one of those men who knew how to get things done. Tall, handsome, and supremely confident, he exuded success. He had made a fortune through his own construction business, and he over-indulged his little girl shamelessly. He nurtured, pro-tected and encouraged her, supported all signs of initiative, took an interest in all that she did and pride in her childish accomplishments. It was her father that imbued the young girl with a lifelong sense that there was nothing she couldn't accomplish, no limits on what she could do, save the one that he alone imposed.

To little Gloria her father was a god; her admiration for him never faltered, even when she began to dimly realize that there was a price for his continued beneficence. For she soon found that although he encouraged her indepen-dence in dealing with others, and blithely ignored her growing recalcitrance toward her mother, he did insist on one thing—her absolute and total submission to his iron will.

John Brennan was a man who took immense pride in his family; an exacting man, whose life was structured and ordered. He could be a warm, caring, and even affec-tionate parent, provided things were done his way. But if there was the slightest hint of defiance on the part of the young girl, punishment was swift and hard. John Brennan believed in corporal punishment, and felt it was his duty as a parent to personally take his impetuous daughter in hand.

Memories of being spanked by her father remained with her to this day. She would come to him as he sat in the wooden kitchen chair, grim and unsmiling. She had to loosen her jeans and shove them down her skinny legs. She remembered laying upended, draped over her father's lap: a skinny, lanky kid, her jeans down around her knees, her pantied bottom exposed. She waited tensely, eyes shut tight, cringing in dread anticipation of an unrelenting spanking so furious it would take her breath away.

Those spankings continued, some would say beyond all propriety, well into her teenage years. The spankings would remain a family secret.

But even worse than the spankings were the times when he cut her off, turning away from her, shutting her out of his life and refusing to speak to her for days at a time, while he sunk into an icy moodiness. She found his rejection to be devastating, much more terrible than the throbbing ache inflicted by his walloping hand, and far worse than the constant sniping of her aloof, distant mother, which she had begun to take for granted.

Growing up very much alone, Gloria had no place to turn but inward. She became introspective and guarded, careful to protect and nurture the tiny flame she carried in her bosom. For she knew she held this inner flame, her secret. It gave her strength and comforted her. It would see her through. And when she inevitably made her tearful submission, and her father looked down to smile on her, that tiny flame flared, flooding her with inner warmth.

And so Gloria grew up, a wiry tomboy whose inner strength hardened even as she developed outwardly into a very pretty young woman. She learned to take full advantage of her father's money and her crisp good looks, two qualities that she came to rely on in making her way in the wider world outside of her family. By college, she had added a veneer of easy feminine charm, and found, somewhat to her surprise, that her attractive, engaging smile drew people to her with very little effort on her part.

Yet for all her superficial warmth, Gloria grew up wary of all human relationships, and especially distrustful of men, her misgivings on that score being amply validated by a brief and ill-advised marriage to a selfish, arrogant musician. That one grand gesture, made in open defiance of her implacable father, ended predictably in disaster. This was the Gloria Brennan that Ali knew, and didn't know.

Decker's gray eyes came back to find her, searching, watching her as she held court. He held her in his unwavering gaze, biding his time, hoping for the opportunity to talk to her alone.

But time passed, and he never saw a chance. It was hopeless. She was constantly surrounded. Finally, with a last look over his shoulder, he went to get himself another drink. And when he returned to his post, she was gone!

Disbelief was followed by a sudden panic at the terrible thought that he'd lost her. Desperate, he shoved his way through the crowded rooms, rushing toward the open glass doors and the deck just beyond. Bounding through the doorway, he caught himself in mid-stride, abruptly applying the brakes.

Incredibly, there she was, standing just a few feet away, her back to him.

She was bending over to light a cigarette. He paused to take a breath, and stood still for a moment, collecting himself, angry at himself for his foolish wild excitement and his rapidly pounding heart. She turned at the sound of his approach, an expectant look on her face.

"Hello, I'm Tommy Decker," he offered, working to keep his voice calm.

"Gloria Brennan," she replied, looking him over before confidently extending an elegant hand and giving him her best winning smile.

CHAPTER TWO

THAT NIGHT AT ALI'S was very much on Decker's mind as he drove to meet Gloria several weeks later. What had impressed him was her forthright, honest manner. Not that there wasn't the usual mutual wariness at first, as they circled like two cautious wrestlers. It was just that she frankly found him attractive, and Gloria didn't believe in small talk. She knew a pickup was obviously on his mind, and that was just fine with her.

And so it was easy for Gloria to return his smile, settle back, and see where the evening went. And when he finally proposed they leave for some quieter place, she promptly suggested her place. And so it was done.

He remembered the strange newness of her bed; the fresh, delicate scent of her sheets. And then Gloria closed on him with the full fury of her pent-up need. She grabbed for him, clutched him to her with burning urgency, scissoring those long, strong legs of hers around his hips and bucking up meet his pumping hips with a fierceness that took his breath away. And yet while she fucked with surprising enthusiasm, Decker couldn't shake the feeling that something was not quite right about the girl. It had all been too pat.

* * *

He had barely finished his drink when she took his hand and abruptly stood up, announcing it was time they went to bed. Taken aback, yet tingling with excitement at the nearness of bedding this dark-haired beauty, he let himself be led into the darkened bedroom. He was disappointed that she didn't bother to turn on the lights, but left him standing there in the middle of the room while she slipped out of her heels and wiggled out of her dress. Her hands went to her pantyhose, and froze there at her waist while she turned to look at him.

"Well, come on, lover. Get undressed," she urged; her tone took on the edge of an order.

She waited until she saw him begin to unbutton his shirt, before turning away to swiftly finish her own undressing. She removed her bra, and skimmed down her underpants, stepping out of them with alacrity so that he managed to get only a glimpse of her nude body in the shadows, before she quickly slipped between the sheets.

Silently, she turned to him, offering up her mouth to be kissed, while at the same time slipping a hand down between their writhing bodies to seek his manhood. At the electric touch of that soft feminine hand groping between his legs, his thickening cock was instantly alerted; all his misgivings vanished. His penis sprang to immediate attention, and a renewed surge of urgency welled up in him as she tightened her fist on his rock-hard penis.

With a surge of body hunger, she pulled him toward her, spreading her scissoring legs, eager to draw him down into her wet softness, letting him feel the urgency of her loins to have his prick inside her. He rolled on top of her hot squirming body, and she wiggled her hips while guiding his prick to her cunt, and then wrapping those athletic legs around his body.

He let himself sink into her, driving his prick right up her slick, silky cunt all the way till his balls smacked against her splayed open crotch, while the impaled woman gurgled, a low animal sound that turned into a wavering groan of deep satisfaction. Immediately, she started bucking, and just as quickly Decker was jolted by a single thrill of intense pleasure that rocketed through him. And a few moments later, Gloria shuddered; a tiny whimper escaped from her tightly pressed lips marking the passage of a perfunctory orgasm. Her thighs fell slackly open, and she lay still, her labored breathing evening out as she got back her equilibrium. Decker had not come, but held himself still within her, as her vagina spasmed in tiny aftershocks on his prick. Then he began to move again, making small tentative thrusts, but she grunted and pushed on his shoulders.

"No. No more now," she whispered. And she wiggled up and slid out from under his dead weight.

Decker rolled over onto his back, his intact erection bathed in love juices, cool upon its sudden exposure to the room's air. The man lay awash with a mixture of curious emotions. He closed his eyes to collect himself as his own breathing evened out. It was not just that he was drained, but that he also felt empty, sadly disappointed, almost as though he had been robbed. He opened his eyes to stare at the dark ceiling, his mind a blank; his penis softened, limp and damp on his thigh.

He felt her stir beside him. Shifting her weight she

raised herself up on one elbow and leaned over him. A swaying breast grazed his arm as she planted a quick dry kiss on his cheek.

"Can you see yourself out, lover?" she cooed in his ear. "I have a busy day tomorrow, and I wouldn't get any sleep if you stayed."

With a final peck on the cheek, she rolled over, turning her back on him. It took Decker a moment to realize—he had been dismissed! He mumbled something about calling her again, but all he got by way of reply from the huddled form was a sleepy grunt.

Incensed, Decker swung his legs over the bed and, flushed with anger, grabbed for his pants. He wanted out, away from her, and as soon as possible. Hurriedly, he pulled on his clothes and, still only half-dressed, his shirt undone, shoes and socks in hand, he stalked from her bedroom.

Outside, the night air was soft and warm. He decided to walk. Jamming his fists deep into his pocket, he broke into a long brisk stride.

* * *

That night was to be played out again and again in what was to become an increasingly frustrating affair with Gloria. At first, he decided that it was simply that she didn't know him very well. The girl was naturally cautious, and she made it clear that she didn't want to get involved. Yet, while she did not exactly encourage him, she never refused a date, and she was always friendly and seemed glad to see him. Later, he decided that she wished to remain detached, valuing her independence above all else, especially her independence where men were concerned. And so their affair had taken on a curiously circumscribed quality, the boundaries carefully laid down.

She insisted their evenings follow a routine, one that inevitably ended with that sort of brief, perfunctory love-making that she seemed to think was quite natural; the whole thing neatly orchestrated, controlled by Gloria Brennan from beginning to end.

Then one night he walked into the bedroom before her, turning on all the lights as he went. She made some lame joke about that, and followed him around the room snapping lights off. Later in bed, when she reached for him, he rolled toward her and slid his cupped hands down up her sleek flanks, inching them around till he was gripping her cheeks and digging his curving fingers into her crack. She squirmed in sudden agitation, but he used his superior weight to pin her down as she struggled, ignoring her murmuring protests, persisting in his intimate exploration till his impertinent fingers found the pinkish rosette he sought. Quite purposely, he extended his index finger to probe Gloria's anus, and got an immediate and vehement reaction.

"No!" she snapped, clamping his wrist, digging into the flesh with her nails, and flinging the offending hand aside.

Immediately, she got a firm grip on his straining erection, and guided him toward her gaping sex, but this time he pulled back. Raising himself up, he straddled her on his knees, looking down at her, just as her eyes snapped wide open. He could see the anger flare in those dark wide eyes. The challenge of her defiance infuriated him.

"Go on! What are you waiting for? Fuck me. Fuck me!" she hissed insistently.

At that curt command, something snapped in the man, and he grabbed her roughly and rolled her over onto her belly before she could react. Surprised by the suddenness of his move, Gloria yelped and struggled to get up onto her elbows, kicking and flailing wildly. She tried to raise herself but Decker was too quick for her, scrambling on top of her struggling body, slithering up her smooth sleek back.

"No! What are you doing?" she hissed between clenched teeth.

But Decker was now filled with his own cold resolve, grimly determined to subdue the woman. Without a word, he got up to straddle her writhing flanks and slid back to sit on her failing legs. A flattened palm on the middle of her back pinned her to the mattress.

"No! No! noooo . . ." she grunted, snapping her head from side to side, and straining to rise up off the mattress.

By now Decker was firmly in the saddle, and he leaned forward and shoved her down with his hand between her shoulder blades, pressing her face in the pillow. He leaned down to bury his face in her soft hair, intoxicated by the clean scent of her perfume.

"Settle down Gloria! I think it's time we got a few things straight between us," he breathed in her ear.

He straightened up and, holding her in place with his extended arm, brought the other hand back to deliver a crisp slap squarely across her bare butt, sending those soft rearmounts wobbling, and getting a yelp of surprised outrage from the helpless woman.

Before she could react, he struck again and again and again, slapping her ass cheeks repeatedly with hard, furious smacks. He was determined to punish her, to spank the willful bitch into submission, and he thoroughly enjoyed the perverse thrill it gave him, savoring the bouncy resiliency of Gloria Brennan's wobbly cheeks, delighting in the jello-like dance of those bouncy mounds under the steady wacking, while the twisting woman shrieked her outrage, and cursed a blue streak.

It was only when her protests grew more feeble, finally turning into whimpered pleas for him to stop, that Decker relented. He gazed down at her heaving, reddened bottom, and gently laid a curved hand on the blushing shapely bottom. Her buttocks clenched, the sides hollowing out, in fearful anticipation of yet another slap. But he simply let his hand rest there, and she gradually relaxed, letting her butt muscles slacken till she lay still, her body limp. Only the slight heaving of her shoulders told him she was sobbing into her pillow.

And now he moved his hand to the back of her head, stroking her, silently petting her. He let it linger there, running his fingers through her rich mane, fingering her silky tresses as he spoke to her. Softly, he tried to explain to her that she had given him no choice: he had to do what he had t o do.

He went on to tell her how incredibly lovely she was; that she had so much to give, if only she'd let herself. It would be tragic waste, he told her, if she kept on this destructive course, chasing the illusion of self-fulfillment and convinced it could be found if only she were even more "liberated." He knew many women like her. Vaguely dissatisfied with life, they searched for someone to blame and, in the end, found it convenient to make men the cause of their discontent. They were, after all, victims.

From there it was a short step to the conclusion that equality of the sexes would right all their wrongs. Most of them never noticed that in their misguided drive for something called equality they gained something but lost something even more precious to their essence.

They were women who denied sex, would allow its expression only in carefully controlled ways, so that it became something mechanical, freely engaged in, provided certain boundaries were kept intact. Limited and proscribed as it was, sex was degraded to simply another biological need, nothing more. Thus they deprived themselves, and their partners, of one of the greatest sources of human pleasure. He hoped she wouldn't let that happen to her.

When his little speech was over he waited to see how she'd respond. Her reply, when it finally came, was muffled by the pillow. Tight-lipped, in a voice dripping with venom, she uttered each word precisely:

"Will you get off me now?"

Stung by her cold fury and frustrated by his own inability to break through, Decker grunted, hauled off and delivered a stinging slap with the flat of his hand, sending those rearmounds juddering once again with his parting shot. She yelped, and kicked her heels up, but kept her face buried in her pillow. He ignored her reaction, dismounted, and climbed down off the bed. Without a word he began to gather up his clothes, making his way through the darkened apartment and out her door, for what he felt was almost certainly the last time.

CHAPTER THREE

DECKER REALLY NEVER gave up hope that she would call; although he kept telling himself it would never happen, he half-hoped that she might call. Then a week went by; two; three; and he worked to convince himself she was out of his life . . . good riddance. It was time to move on.

Still, he couldn't get the lovely brunette out of his mind. Thoughts of her naked continued to creep into his head at odd times: images of that silken hair fanning down over her bare shoulders, those long devastating legs, her soft warm body squirming under his in the darkened bedroom, and, of course, that shapely bottom, the taut bounciness of those upturned rearmounds dancing so delightfully under his walloping hand.

A month went by, and he had given up all hope, but unbelievably, there was a message from her on his answering machine when he came home one night. She suggested they meet for dinner in a place they had gone before. She hoped they might get together and talk, she added rather cryptically. The tremendous rush of elation was immediately followed by an inner warning. His mind raced furiously, considering the many possibilities. He would have to proceed very, very carefully.

She had, of course, taken a large step in contacting him. The initiative was clearly hers; that was as it had to be. Still, even though it was her invitation, it would be necessary at the outset to keep her from reestablishing control of their relationship. Even the little things were important.

He called her at her office, knowing he would get her secretary, and left a message. He countered with lunch instead of dinner. He would be at Santoro's at noon. When the secretary asked if she should have Ms. Brennan return his call, he told her there was no need to reply. Gloria would understand: He would be there; he expected her to be there too.

Santoro's was noisy and bustling at lunchtime, hardly the place for an intimate talk. Decker had chosen it purposely; a light and airy place, with wicker furnishings, potted palms, polished wood trim with brass fittings, and tall windows which angled up to form frosted skylights over the front of the place. It seemed spacious even when crowded with the hurried businessmen who were the usual lunchtime clientele.

Gloria sat across from him, looking cool and proper in a trim pinstriped business suit. The dark severity of her lawyer's outfit gave her a conservative air, dramatically contrasted by the luxurious abundance of inky black hair she wore loose, tumbling down to her shoulders in a riot of blatant sensual excess.

Decker gazed fondly on that lovely hair. It was her hair that reminded him of Marilyn. Marilyn was his cousin from long ago and far away. A few years older than he, she had stayed with him and his mother for several years while he was in high school and she attended the local college. He was a skinny, awkward kid, a 15-year-old who walked around with a permanent erection, a teenaged caricature of his adult self, and one he vehemently denied on those occasions when he came across a high school photo. In a way it was true that the shy, introverted teenager had become someone else, since Decker had worked to recreate himself, gone about the business of building an adult version step by step right after he got out of the Navy.

He thought of Marilyn now, as he stared admiringly at Gloria's radiant hair, remembered how her mysterious female presence had touched his drab home and brought with it the first glimmers of sexual excitement.

He would watch her covertly, this strange female creature, as she ran about the house, half-dressed, getting ready for a date. He would linger in the hallway, so that she ran into him when she came out of the bathroom, flushed and warm shower, her naked body clad in nothing but a thin silk wrapper. True, the silvery pink robe covered her modestly from chest to knees, but tightly sashed it was thin enough to allow the boy to just make out the curves of her young breasts and the nubby bumps of those pointy nipples she sported.

He found himself spying on the girl whenever he got the chance. Sometimes when she was getting dressed, she might neglect to completely close the door. He watched and waited for those rare opportunities. And when he was lucky enough to find she'd left it open just a crack, he would quickly position himself so he could get a glimpse of her as she crossed the room dressed in nothing but her panties and bra. He would creep as close as he dared to secretly watch the dark-haired girl gathering up her things, pulling on a tank top, slipping into her jeans, and all the while his growing erection throbbed with a desperate ache of longing.

Once he saw her padding around her room in nothing but a loose top that barely covered the bright pink thong she had on. Her back to the door, she bent over to pick up her socks, causing the top to ride up her arched back, and inadvertently giving her observer a choice view of her tight young butt, her cheeks left deliciously exposed by the sexy thong. Suddenly, for some inexplicable reason, the bending girl turned to look over her shoulder, and caught her cousin redhanded, standing in the doorway—his hand on his crotch! Decker flushed, horribly embarrassed to be caught spying. But to his surprise, she didn't raise hell with him. In fact, she didn't seem very surprised to see him standing there, didn't even seem to mind that he was staring at her at all. She just gave him a curious look, as if she were wrestling with some decision, and then a smile creased her lips, a little knowing half-smile of secret satisfaction, and she straightened up and very slowly closed the door. He was relieved and elated, pleased that this older girl was so wonderfully tolerant of him; he was so very grateful she hadn't laughed at his weakness or scolded him like a little boy with his hand caught in the cookie jar.

That night he waited as long as he decently could, before telling his mother that he was tired and was going to bed early. Once safely behind the locked door of his bedroom, he rummaged through his closet to retrieve his cache of dirty pictures. His very favorite pictures that he came back to again and again.

He got on the bed, opened his belt, shoved his jeans and his briefs down to his knees, freeing his massive erection which sprang up, hard and ready. He quickly flipped through the pictures for the one he wanted. He grabbed his cock and began a slow masturbation. Before him was a photograph of a tall willowy blonde, stripped completely naked, and held up on her tiptoes by her hand-cuffed wrists which were tied high overhead. But when he closed his eyes, and his fist tightened to begin pulling on his cock, it was not the image of the blonde in bondage, but one of his dark-haired cousin, bending over, her bare ass jutting back at him, that gave him the rush that drove him on.

He knew his cousin's bedroom was off-limits. But sometimes, when he was home alone, he would go in there anyway, just to stand there and look around, tingling with the strangeness of the room, the exciting smells. He needed to touch her things, to peer in the drawers of her clothes chest, curious about this fascinating female in their midst. He went for the drawer where she kept her underwear, riffing through the silky things, fingering a slippery pair of lacy silver panties.

It gave him a deliciously secret thrill, just being there, in the privacy of her room, handling the things she wore next to her body. A few minutes of this and he was powerfully turned on, so hot and bothered that he'd race back to his own room to beat off. One day he plunged a hand down the front of his jeans to grab his cock as he was examining her lingerie, and the crazy idea came to him of jacking off right there on her bed! Hastily, he grabbed a pair of panties, opened his jeans, and shoved them down, climbed up on her bed, and very carefully rubbed himself along the satiny bedspread. The feeling was indescribably delicious but he couldn't keep it up, or there would surely be stains on the spread that would be hard to explain. So he rolled over onto his back, wrapped her panties around his cock, got a solid grip, closed his eyes, and began pumping his fist in slow steady strokes, surrendering to the dreamy feelings flooding up in him.

Suddenly, a noise startled him, and his eyes flew open to regard his cousin standing in the doorway. She was looking down on him with that same half-smile he had seen before.

It turned out that, although she was considerably more experienced in sexual matters than he was, she had never seen a boy masturbating, and she told him it was all right for him to continue; more than all right, she wanted him to continue, and she hoped he wouldn't mind if she watched.

Thus began for Decker a wild, passion-drenched affair, carried on right under his mother's nose, with a warm and generous girl, a helpful cousin who was older and seemed so much wiser, and all too willing to teach the sex-crazed adolescent a thing or two.

He thought of her fondly now, as he studied Gloria Brennan across the table from him, idly wondering what kind of underwear she had on under the severe business suit she wore. Today, she seemed unusually quiet and subdued. The line of her painted lips was drawn taut, and when she looked at him, there was a somber, haunted look in her deep dark eyes. But mostly she avoided looking at him, preferring the passing world outside the window, the menu, the other patrons, anything to avoid Decker's frankly curious gaze. For his part, he was polite, friendly, if a trifle distant, forcing himself to play a patient, waiting game, working to hold down his soaring hopes. Like casual acquaintances, they exchanged only a few words, while the waitress fussed with the menus. But once their coffee had arrived, he settled back and eyed her up expectantly, letting the silence build.

Gloria was plainly uncomfortable under his curious gaze. She shifted uneasily and then leaned forward with a conspiratorial air, as though she were afraid they might be overheard in the crowded restaurant. She ducked her head, and studied her long curving fingers as they closed around her coffee cup, carefully considering what she was about to say. And when, with head still lowered, she finally began, it was in a halting voice, hesitant, and uncharacteristically tentative.

"You see, Tommy, the thing is . . . well, I've been thinking about us, and that night you . . . well, the last time we were together."

She looked up at him from under her fine dark lashes scanning his face. But she was met with only a polite blank stare from those cool gray eyes. She took a breath and continued.

"You know, when you . . . It's just that I. . . . I dunno . . . I just . . ." she stammered. Fascinated, Decker watched the pretty woman practically squirming in discomfort, but he did nothing to help her, just sat there, waiting.

She took a deep breath and continued. "What I mean is . . . I think about you a lot, what we did the last time we were together. This isn't easy to say." She brought those big brown eyes up to meet his. "Damnit! You sonovabitch, I can't get you out of my mind." The words tumbled out in a desperate hiss. "It's driving me crazy!" she managed to add in a husky whisper. He waited, but she said no more, but sat looking down with eyes on the white linen tablecloth.

"Why, Gloria, I had no idea! You really liked it, didn't you? What a naughty girl you are! It turned you on, having that pretty bottom of yours warmed, didn't you? Now, c'mon, 'fess up," he teased.

He studied her lowered head and waited. And then he saw the little nod, barely perceptible.

"By God, I knew it! It turned you on, didn't it?" He crowed, having guessed her secret.

He sat there with a look of pleased triumph, that smug grin that Gloria found insufferable. The man could hardly contain his glee. She despised him for it, for his enjoying this, her humiliating confession. She kept her head lowered, curled her lower lip, bit down on it with a row of even white teeth. And he waited.

She realized she was being forced to tell him that she was secretly obsessed with thoughts of being spanked, of laying across a man's lap, of having her bottom bared, exposing her ass to him, to his eyes, to his strong masculine hands. How could she tell him about the throb of lust that went through her at the thought of having her bottom fondled by his hands; of the impact of the sharp sting, and the warm and cozy afterglow that followed, that left her tingling with arousal? Yet, that was precisely what he was waiting for.

Gloria glanced sideways and leaned across the table. Decker felt the tingle of excitement rising up in him, but he forced himself to relax, to settle back, to watch and wait. Finally, she looked up at him and continued in a hoarse whisper.

"It's the thought of being held down like that, helpless, while I'm being . . . spanked," she managed to get out in a choked voice. A delicious shiver ran through her at the final hushed word, and she hastily ducked her head. She scanned his face, but he just sat there with an unwavering stare, a polite, thin-lipped smile on his face.

Taking a deep breath, she forced herself to go on.

"Some days it's terrible," she admitted. "It doesn't matter what I'm doing . . . sitting through some meeting at work, and not knowing what's going on 'cause I'm thinking only of you. The other day, I was standing in the kitchen, fixing dinner, when suddenly the thought of you, of us, with me over your knee, it flashed through my mind, and I forgot what I was doing, and burned the sauce. The whole idea makes me go all weak in the knees, just thinking it," she confessed in a hushed voice.

And now she sat there burning with embarrassment, angry at the man for forcing this public confession of her weakness. Yet she also felt an undeniable tingling. It excited her, to make such intimate disclosures to this man who sat there in this crowded restaurant, calm, implacable, waiting for her to tell him everything.

Her confession that day in Santoro's broke through the unspoken barrier that had been between them. Now, they understood one another, and whatever happened, things could never be the same between them. By this one act, Gloria had set the stage for a new game, one that Decker would play according to his own rules. He understood what had happened perfectly, and now he decided to put her newfound attitude to the test.

He let her sit there in silence for several long minutes. Her was head bowed, eyes on the tablecloth; he studied the top of her shiny black hair. Then he told her what she must do.

After work on Friday, she was to go straight to his place. They would spend the weekend at his apartment. First, however, they would have to do a little shopping. He paused to pick up the bill, and started to get up.

But she demurred, weakly protesting that she couldn't go shopping now, she was due back at the office for a meeting. He brushed that aside. She could call the office and tell them she was held up. With that he rose to leave, and Gloria dug out her cell phone.

* * *

That afternoon, he took her to shopping. He had in mind certain exclusive boutiques, shops that specialized in sexy lingerie.

Decker quite enjoyed himself, picking out the most intimate things for her to wear. There was a endless array of feminine undergarments: filmy nylon, slippery silks, and smooth, slick satins. They waded through piles of skimpy underwear, wispy things made of the sheerest fabrics. There were flimsy brassieres of fine mesh adorned with delicate embroidery; camisoles, chemises, and slips made of shiny metallic satin and edged with generous panels of fine lace. He gathered up handfuls of panties; creamy briefs edged in frothy lace; thin pastel panties in a variety of colors; low-riding bikini bottoms made of pure silk. He held up a thong for her to inspect, remarking that it would be lovely addition to her wardrobe, allowing her gorgeous bottom to hang out to be admired while she pranced around the bedroom for him in a pair of heels. She blushed and turned aside, but he pursued her, insisting she wear the sexy underwear when she went back to the office, under her staid business suit. He chose several pairs of tinted tights in blues and maroons and greens and browns, and sheer body stockings in nude and smoky gray, and a half-dozen pair of long black nylons, thigh-highs with wide topbands of elasticized lace.

He took his time, carefully fingering the exquisite silks, the fine satins, examining each gossamer scrap in detail, and inviting her comments in a clear loud voice. A black bustier caught his eye. He made her hold it up to her body so he might get some idea of how she would look in it. Other customers couldn't help noticing, and he seemed glad of it. But most often his little game was played in front of a slightly embarrassed salesgirl who struggled to keep a strained smile on her face. Then he would make some lewd remark, and when she blushed furiously he would laugh, and order the girl to wrap it up.

By three o'clock Gloria was back at her office, feeling

slightly giddy, confused, caught up in a whirl. She felt like a schoolgirl with her first crush on the boy next door. It had all happened so fast. Whenever she thought of modeling her new underwear for him, an electric thrill shot secretly through her. She was always aware that under her business suit, the tight black thong snuggled between the cheeks of her ass, and the thoughts of parading around in front of him, clad only in those sexy panties turned her insides to jelly. For the first time in years, she felt totally alive. She couldn't wait for the weekend, counted the hours.

But then by Friday, she began to have her doubts. What had she done? And more importantly, what had she let herself in for, by agreeing to spend the weekend with him? She really didn't know all that much about him.

She couldn't concentrate on work at all, and as five o'clock neared, her misgivings grew and panic began to set in. She could still call the whole thing off. It would be easy to say no. She owed him nothing. Yet, something kept her from saying no. There was really no way out. Gloria knew it. She would take a taxi to his apartment that night because she simply had no choice.

CHAPTER FOUR

THAT DAY AT SANTORO'S, as Decker sat listening to a profoundly humiliated Gloria admit to her deepest desires, he had to struggle to keep the rising sense of elation from finding expression on his face. He knew well that lustful longing she spoke of, knew the sexual obsession that gripped her, for he had experienced the very same throbbing ache of desire. For that memorable night was never far from his own thoughts; it intruded upon him at odd moments . . . in the very same way. Yet he never told her that. Wildly pleased to hear this beautiful girl admit to her darkest desires, he kept his expression carefully neutral. With each halting word, he knew that the impulse he acted on that night had been the right one.

So now it was with a burst of confidence that he quickly took charge, shepherding the girl through their whirlwind shopping tour. And when he finally deposited her back at her office, he knew there was no doubt—she would be there: his place, Friday night.

But the next morning, he was no longer so sure. Like Gloria, he spent a long agonizing day, tense and keyed up, his nerves tingling in anticipation, unable to concentrate. His thoughts were dominated by erotic images of the dark-haired girl, her naked body twisting under his punishing hand. His feelings oscillated wildly between an elated sense of triumph and the dread of despair. He worried that he had badly overplayed his hand, foolishly had gone too far, and now he would lose this proud beauty forever.

Shaking off his fears, Decker made his preparations with meticulous care. He placed his black naugahyde arm-chair in the center of the room, turning it to face the door. Carefully, he arranged the track lighting so that two narrow beams were sent angling down to form a halo of light on the thick Persian rug just in front of the black chair. Next, he showered and shaved, emerging from the bathroom to wrap his nakedness in a plush velour robe. Padding around the room, he turned off all the other lights, unlocked the door, and settled into his easy chair to light a cigar, and await the woman he needed so desperately.

Seven o'clock came . . . and went. Then 7:05, and then 7:10; Decker's fears wildly escalating with each passing minute. And then he heard her light knock on his door.

He kept his soaring elation out of his voice, as he called for her to enter.

The door opened a crack, and Gloria slipped furtively into the apartment. She wore a fashionable leather coat and matching gloves, and nervously clutched a small overnight bag. Under the large-brimmed hat, he could see that face was pale, her lips tightly drawn. Her move-ments seemed hesitant, unsure, as she closed the door and hovered in the shadows of the doorway.

"Lock the door, then take off your hat and coat, and come over here . . . where I can see you," he called from the chair; his voice, dry, but with an edge of authority.

She removed the hat, gave a quick toss to her hair. Then slipped off her coat. For a moment she stood there, unsure, her things in her hands. He gestured toward the closet by the door, and she placed her hat, coat, and bag there. Then she came into the room, entering the circle of light, to stand before his chair. He studied her sharply dressed figure as she stood before him with hands loosely at her sides, her head tilted downward, supple shadows masking her features, the abundance of her radiant hair floating around her face like a dark cloud.

Decker was inordinately pleased to see that she had followed his instructions and dressed in her business clothes: the neatly tailored charcoal suit, the high-buttoned white blouse with its tunic collar, crisp and cut like a man's shirt, tinted dark nylons and heels. He let her stand there in silence, taking his time, appraising her tense figure from the crown of her dark hair to the pointed toes of her shiny patent leather pumps.

"You're late," he muttered, tight-lipped, glancing up to study her exquisite face.

"I know. I'm sorry but . . ." she mumbled, her eyes on the rug.

"You're late," he repeated. "Now, get undressed." The words were casual, matter-of-fact. They sent a shudder of lust through the tense woman.

She looked down at him, and Decker found himself captivated once more by those lustrous dark eyes, beautiful eyes, framed with long dark lashes. And as he looked into those expressive eyes, he saw them soften. The usual bright brittleness seemed to melt away. The look she gave him now penetrated right through him, thrilled him to the core, told him more eloquently than words could ever do that the woman was his. She would do his bidding, place herself totally in his hands.

"Go on, take your clothes off, all of them. I want you naked." His voice came out husky and strained.

Now he saw those wonderful eyes glaze over into surrender, her bright-eyed alertness fading to a soft passivity. She visibly straightened and moved as if in a trance.

Without a word, she brought her hands up to her lapels. Decker watched the scene unfold as in slow motion: those narrow hands rose up, the long fingers with their gleaming red tips worked to slip off the jacket, peeling it back to free one shoulder, then the other, twisting out of the jacket and letting it drop down her extended arms in back, till she could pull it free. For a moment she held the garment, uncertainly. Then, finding nowhere to set it, she simply let it drop to the floor. Now, the hands went to the button of the collar of the plain white blouse she wore.

"No!" He stopped the hands in mid-air. She gave him an inquisitive look.

"The skirt . . . first, take off your skirt." The hushed order caused her to quiver.

The elegant hands obediently quit the blouse and dropped down to reach behind, undoing the catch and lowering the little zipper at the back of the skirt. Bending forward slightly, her head lowered, she began to work the narrow skirt down over the cradle of her hips.

"Look at me. You are to keep looking at me while you undress."

She raised her face, and he saw the look of acquiescence, the softness that said she had yielded to his quiet commands.

With her eyes still on his, she gathered two fistfuls of material at each side and tugged the skirt down, bringing her ankles together and gave a girlish shimmy. Holding herself erect, she bent her knees in a half squat and rode the crumpled skirt the rest of the way down her nyloned legs till the skirt ringed her ankles. Then, still keeping her eyes on Decker's face as instructed, she straightened up and lifted first one foot, then the other, delicately stepping out of her collapsed skirt. The seated man opened his legs. His swelling cock stirred expectantly when he saw the pointed-toed shoe nudge the discarded skirt to one side.

He smiled as he recognized the half-slip she had on—a narrow sheath of shiny black satin. Edged with a wide border of delicate lace, the short undergarment hung down just to her knees. She automatically reached up under the blouse to take off her slip. But as she hooked her thumbs in the waistband, she caught herself, paused, and gave the seated man an inquisitive look. Decker nodded, and Gloria proceeded, leaning forward to draw the black slip down her hips till gravity could take over. The slippery undergarment dropped straight down her legs to collapse in a satin heap at her feet. She stepped out of the inky puddle and nudged it aside, to join the little pile of discarded clothing accumulating at her feet.

As Gloria straightened up, she was suddenly stuck by an acute awareness of her situation. She had a flashing image—how she must look as she stood there, skirtless, under the glare of the twin spotlights, slowly peeling off her clothes, a stripper performing for her male audience of one. The intense thrill electrified her, bringing a delicious shiver of feminine pride in its wake. With an imperious toss of her magnificent mane, the tall woman straightened to her full impressive height, squaring her shoulders and widening her bold stance, brazenly inviting the man to look, to admire.

Holding herself perfectly erect, she waited—a study in dramatic contrasts: the classic beauty of her pale face, the high-chiseled cheekbones, the equine nose and wide, etched lips, painted in a wet crimson. Those finely drawn features of hers were framed by the deep ebony tresses, loose waves of jet black silk that cascaded down over the pure white of the loose blouse which hung straight on her tall, lean body. The blouse's hem barely layered her brand new panties, lacy black panties with high-arching leg-bands that left her haunches and a generous band of suc-culent thighflesh exposed as the eye fell to the wide topbands of her shimmering black nylons. Decker admired those splendid, mouth-watering thighs before letting his eyes trail down to lovingly caress the exquisite feminine curves of Gloria's tall, lean legs, unbroken lines tapering from thighs to ankles to end at the tips of the gleaming high-heeled pumps she still wore.

Decker smiled to himself when he saw that proud toss she gave to that rich mane. Gloria was a good-looking woman, and like most beautiful women, she knew it. Though she had grown up acutely aware of her budding beauty, and well knew the effect it had on men, this was not the haughty gesture of a conceited, self-centered woman. On the contrary, it was something else—a frank display of feminine pride, of being a woman who was desirable, and wanted by a man who would take her.

And for Decker, seated with bare feet widely planted, and a full erection tenting his robe, there had never been a more desirable sight. He felt the upwelling of lust, the power surging through to further stiffen his upright prick. Insatiable, his greedy eyes swept up and down her par-tially clad form till they were arrested by the sheer ele-gance of those tall legs—the splendid architecture of those sleek-muscled, dancer's legs, set in their rigid stance, high heels planted several inches apart. He yearned to reach out, to touch those nyloned lengths, to stroke them, to run his hands up along those marvelous sleek contours; but he forced himself to wait.

He was uncomfortably warm now, his brow sheened with sweat. His straining penis was fully aroused and stood up rigidly. Stiffened with lusty male power, it poked obscenely against the front of the loosely belted robe, threatening to break through the flaps at the slightest movement. Seated in the semi-darkness just outside the circle of light, he wondered if she could see the obvious state of his arousal. He moved his hand in the shadows to brush aside the flaps of the robe, letting his jutting manhood spring free. He saw her eyes follow the movement in the shadows; saw her moist lips part at the unmistakable evidence of his naked desire.

"The blouse," he croaked. His mouth had gone suddenly dry.

She looked down on him and held herself still, but the hands continued to move as if with a life of their own, mechanically unbuttoning the cuffs. He watched as her fingers went to the collar, and proceeded down, undoing each button in turn, working her way down the front of the blouse while the lengthening narrow triangle in her wake exposed her creamy chest banded with the sexy black brassiere he had bought for her. She slipped the blouse back off her shoulders, pulled her arms free, and let the garment fall with studied indifference.

Gloria's sleek front was now revealed. Her breasts, two neatly sized handfuls, were tautly rounded curves, bulging slightly in the snug confines of sheer net cups so prettily decorated with filigreed lace. The shadowy disks of Gloria's large dusky nipples peeked through the gauzy film. Below the bra was a satiny midriff, smooth and even down to a flat belly, a shallow navel and pointy hips upon which rested her low-slung panties.

Decker quickly licked his lips. "Take the bra off," he managed to get out.

Leaning over to reach up in back, Gloria undid the

clasp of the bra strap, brushed the flimsy shoulder straps down, and gathered up the sagging cups in her hands, as her taut breasts fell free, juddered and shimmied as they settled into place. The lacy tangle of straps and cups was added to the growing pile of clothing at her feet.

Decker's eyes followed the seductive sway of her those unfettered tits as she straightened up: two uptilted, slightly flattened mounds, sporting crinkled nipples embedded in wide, dusky auerolae. As he studied her softly rounded tits he thought he saw the tips stiffen under his frank admiration, the disks expanding, the tips protruding before his very eyes.

He savored the long sweep of that splendid torso, the finely etched collarbone, the sculpted contours of her smooth upperchest, the sleek lines shading into the gentle slopes that melded, in turn, to the gently sloping top curves of her close-set breasts. His eyes followed the narrow precise valley of her cleavage as the lines fanned out below into the delicious undercurves, and then they dropped further to trace the faint outline of the lower edge of her ribcage, scanning along the shallow indentation of her hourglass waist, and over the silken midriff, the smooth flesh drawn taut between the ridges of her flaring hips; hips that were still spanned by the pair of sexy black underpants black, low-slung with a shiny satin gusset that nicely molded her gently mounded pubis.

"Come here," he breathed.

She took a single, hesitant step.

"Closer."

The pointed toes of her shoes took one step closer, stopping precisely at the spot he pointed to, just between his widespread legs. Decker could no longer resist the burning need to get his hands on her. His outstretched hand trembled as he curved it around one thigh, sliding it up, gripping the smooth, silky, nyloned column till he heard her gasp in a sharp intake of breath. And then he pulled her loins closer, tightening his grip, savoring the solid feel of her firmly packed nylon.

The tall brunette's eyelids fluttered down and she swayed, tottering forward on her heels. When he fitted his curved hand to her thigh and tightened his curled fingers, she closed her eyes and bit down on her curled lower lip to keep from crying out.

She arched back as, holding her by the leg, he drew her loins to him, bending down to move within inches of her pantied sex. The crotch of the lacy panties was reinforced by a wedge of slick nylon; the silky fabric pulled taut, plastered to the soft bulge of the woman's gently-mounded vulva.

As he brought his face to her crotch Decker's nostrils flared with the unmistakable smell of a woman in heat, the musky, heady scent filled his nostrils as he closed on her sex and buried his face between her thighs. He pressed into the wet crotch of her panties, moist with the telltale strain of feminine juices. He inhaled her scent deeply, then pulled back to look up at the swaying girl. Gloria stood with eyes closed, hands at her sides, her body held rigid with tension as the man closed on her damp womanhood. Her moist lips were slightly parted and her breathing was shallow, her breasts rising and falling in gentle undulations. She sensed his hungry eyes on her sex, could almost feel his desire for her body, and she was aware of the answering lusty need in her loins. There was a heaviness in her breasts. Her swollen nipples tingled with excitement. She could almost feel herself getting wet between the legs.

Decker still held her by the stockinged leg, but now he shoved his cupped hand up to press the edge against her wet crotch. Gloria sucked in a sharp breath through clenched teeth. Her thighs spasmed instinctively, tightening on the male intruder. He held his hand there, feeling her heat, her wetness, patiently waiting for her thigh muscles to slacken. When they relaxed he twisted his hand palm upward to cup her pantied sex and fondle the soft pussy folds through the thin silk. Gloria groaned, swaying like a reed in the wind. Extending a thumb he pressed between the silk-encased folds, seeking her hidden clitoris while he kept manipulating her pussy in a slow, deep rub. The fleshy heel of his palm massaged the fleshy pad of her pubis, while his curling his fingers dug up into the labia, forcing the silken strip up into her cleft.

An abrupt grunt escaped Gloria's tight-pressed lips; she craned up and backward, arching her back in a deep bow, and tossing back her glorious mane. Like a big cat in heat, she savored his caress, twisting sensuously, arching up while her lover's fingers toyed with her moist pussy lips through the slick, damp nylon. Decker glanced upward and was surprised to find her looking down on him, watching his hand through eyes that had narrowed into dark, gleaming slits. Intently watching her face, he squeezed her furry vulva, moving his hand in a slow circular massage. Gloria's long lashes fluttered seductively, as her half-lidded eyes slid closed once more, and she slipped into dreamy reverie. She seemed to purr, luxuriating in the warm waves of pleasure radiating from the firm masculine hand that kept up its slow fondling of her needy sex. Decker could feel her wetness, the incredible heat his hand was generating in her captured womanhood.

"You like this, don't you Gloria?" he asked in a teasing voice. "Does it feel good, having your pussy petted like this?"

"Mmmmmm," she muttered dreamily, arching back with feline grace while his loving hand worked its wonderful magic between her legs.

"Say it!" he hissed.

"Oh . . . yes, yes," she mumbled, "It feels good . . . sooooo good," her voice broke, husky with emotion.

Her passion-choked words fired Decker's simmering lust. He jumped up abruptly, startling the dreamy-eyed woman who flinched at the sudden movement. Clamping his hands on her naked shoulders he walked her backward a few steps and then pressed down, forcing her to her knees. Submissively, Gloria lowered herself before him so that his upstanding prick presented itself at rigid attention just inches from her face. She licked her lips nervously, and took a deep breath, tingling with anticipation and eager to do what he wanted her to do. She went to reach for him with both hands.

But Decker surprised her. Suddenly, he turned his back on her, unbelting the robe, and letting it slip off his shoulders and fall to the floor, presenting her with his naked backside. He leaned over the chair, gripping the arms and lowering his head toward the seat, so as to offer his outthrust butt to the kneeling girl.

For a moment she knelt there, uncomprehending, paralyzed by uncertainty as she stared at the hard-muscled, mannish buttocks. He turned to look down over his shoulder at the woman on her knees.

"Well, what are you waiting for? You know what to do. Go on, Gloria, kiss it! Kiss my ass! Use your lips and mouth and tongue. Get your tongue in there and do me, baby" he ordered impatiently.

His lewd words brought home the full realization of what he wanted her to do. She had heard that some people liked that sort of thing, but she found the thought of it vaguely disgusting. She sat stiffly staring at the dark narrow crack before her eyes, unable to bring herself to perform the obsequious act.

Suddenly she felt that he was further humiliating her, ordering her around, treating her like his personal whore.

She felt a flare of rebellion. Still kneeling upright, she shifted back to sit on her heels, determined not to comply with the man's perverse desires.

For a moment longer he held the pose when he slowly rose up and turned to face her, his stiff erection prominent. Gloria knelt with head lowered, eyes on the carpet, and his lips tightened grimly as he noted her mute refusal.

"Gloria, you're going to have to learn to do what I tell you," he said, shaking his head sadly.

The bowed head didn't move.

"Yes, I'm disappointed in you. I though you were a good girl, good little Gloria. But good girls listen, and they obey. Now bad girls, they're something else. Bad girls disobey, and bad girls get punished for their disobedience until they learn to behave. I'm afraid Gloria, you've been a bad girl. And you know what that means."

An erotic shiver knifed through the kneeling girl.

Now he slipped back into his robe, but left it hanging open, his manhood swaying before him. He took his seat in the big black armchair. Then he silently beckoned her over to him. She rose to her feet, and found herself walking to him, to stand where he pointed, right before him, her eyes cast down, humbly waiting for her punishment like some naughty schoolgirl.

"Tell me, Gloria," he asked, looking up at her, "when you were a little girl, did your parents ever spank you?"

She closed her eyes and nodded dumbly.

"Really! Well. I'll be damned!" Decker couldn't help smiling. "Well, in that case, you're probably long overdue. Now get that ass of yours over here," he ordered brusquely, pointing to his lap. Her eyes followed his pointing finger. The robe had fallen open across his legs, baring his strong thighs and his proudly erect prick.

With heightened feelings, a curious mixture of dread and excitement, the tall brunette found herself moving to comply. With dreamlike movements she submissively draped her lissome form over the man's naked thighs, assuming the classic position without a word. Decker savored the delicious warmth of her soft naked body, the press of a solid hip against his straining manhood as she shifted into position.

He could only guess at the thoughts that were going through Gloria's inverted head as she lay there, her long lean body stretched out, legs angling down one side, head and shoulders down the other. But when she gave a tiny squirm as an uncontrollable shiver rippled through her body, he was certain that she too felt the sense of rising excitement. Just the thought of spanking had turned her on! For Gloria, to be lying across a man's lap, offering up her bottom for a severe spanking, was profoundly humiliating, and deeply satisfying—both at the same time. Just the thought of being spanked like a schoolgirl by a masterful man electrified her with a deliciously wicked, indescribable thrill!

CHAPTER FIVE

GLORIA BRENNAN FOUND herself, unbelievably, stretched out on her belly over Tommy Decker's lap, every fiber of her body tingling with keen anticipation. Her inverted head and shoulders fell down one side so that her cascading hair swept the rug. Her breasts hung softly against Decker's left leg, while the rounded contours of her pantied behind jutted out over his right leg. Her magnificent legs, still sheathed in their thigh-high stockings, were pressed tightly together to form a straight line that angled downward so that her pointy-toed pumps dug into the thick pile of the carpet.

Decker took his time, arranging the passive girl just the way he wanted. Shifting her dead weight, he reached under her to capture her tits, lifting her up enough to tuck them under her so she lay with those warm cuddly mounds mashed against his hairy thighs. He urged her to bend her knees, bringing her legs up so he could slip off her heels.

Even though he was terribly excited, his straining penis raging for satisfaction, he made an effort to move slowly and deliberately, determined to take his time and thoroughly enjoy every minute of what he had dreamed about—returning to Gloria's splendid bottom to administer a proper spanking. And so he took a moment to savor the mouth-watering sight she presented, her extended body half-naked in sexy black nylons and panties. The seat of the panties was pulled taut, tightly packed with those plump rearmounds that threatened to escape from the high-cut legsbands that arched up to bisect her cheeks, leaving exposed their smiling undercurves. The narrow strip banding her hips left bare the high fullness of her naked haunches, one of which rested solidly against his upright penis. He smiled to contemplate that lovely ass—that enticing bottom served up so nicely for his edification and enjoyment.

He brought up a hand to lay it gently on her bottom, splaying his fingers to span the twin cheeks. Her pantied butt clenched in instinctive reaction, and his smile widened. But when she realized that he seemed content, for the moment, to merely caress her bottom through the thin panties, the hardened buttocks went slack. Decker spent a moment rubbing the thin nylon all over the wobbly mounds with his fingertips, fondling and squeezing, happily playing with Gloria's delightful ass. With trembling hands he reached for the elastic waistband, and then hesitated, changing his mind. Now he brought his other hand up and with both hands, slipped his fingers inside the legsbands at each side. He slid his fingers up either side of her crack, forcing the twisted nylon strip into that narrow valley, baring the jutting mounds to his gaze. All this masculine attention to her bottom was getting to Gloria. Unable to keep still, she shifted uneasily in his lap. He curled his fingers around one cheek, digging into the crack, poking the silky strip deep between the exposed clenching cheeks.

Then, clasping her hips with both hands, he slipped his thumbs through the waistband in back, and tugged upward on the tautly stretched panties, forcing the strip of twisted nylon even deeper into her cleft, and getting a guttural grunt from the inverted head that hung down over his legs. Still not satisfied, he clutched a handful of the waistband in back and yanked up again, and again, till the narrow gusset was pulled up tight, embedded deeply in her valley. Each abrupt tug brought a short tight-lipped grunt and tiny jerk of the hips from the laid out woman.

Now, entirely pleased with his arrangement, he let his hand rest on her newly bared ass with a proprietary air. Her relished the feel of her: the silken smooth, hard curves, so unspeakably perfect. He couldn't resist the temptation to bend down and plant a single kiss just on the crown of each exposed cheek. Gloria sighed and twitched eagerly at the delightful touch of the man's lips on her naked behind. He affectionately patted that upturned bottom, and when the taut cheeks clenched once more in instinctive defense, he couldn't help smiling to himself. She was fearful of what was to come. That was good. He would let her apprehension build while he enjoyed himself playing with Gloria Brennan's superb bottom.

Cupping a hand, he lovingly caressed those pert mounds, admiring their perfect symmetry, the satiny smoothness of the rounded contours, the deep division bisecting them, all lewdly accented by the thong he had made out of her twisted panties. As he lovingly rubbed and massaged those pliant mounds, the tense woman stirred with growing impatience. Laid out across his lap in the humiliating position of a naughty schoolgirl, feeling the heat of his thighs, the conspicuous feel of his rigid manhood pressing boldly against her hip, and now the dreamy caress of his firm masculine hand on her ass, Gloria could not keep still. She wriggled her hips, and as he lovingly caressed her ass, a plaintive whimper escaped through her tightly pressed lips.

The girl's seductive squirming sent another surge of lust through Decker's already taut prick. He clamped a hand on her ass, squeezing the soft pliant cheek till his clenching fingers dug painfully in. Gloria yelped, kicking up her heels, as her head snapped back. Twisting in his viselike grip, she mumbled a series of pleading *noooos*. But he ignored her entreaties. He wanted to punish that impertinent bottom of hers. With grim determination, he mauled her butt, grabbing handfuls of ass and viciously tightening his grip while the tormented female wriggled in agony on his lap. When he finally eased up on her, she lay there gasping, her breath coming in ragged gulps, her upturned ass burning with an angry red tinge.

The sight galvanized Decker into action. Wildly excited, he snatched at the waistband of her underpants and yanked viciously, tearing them down her long haunches in one clean sweep. Leaving the damp, twisted scrap stretched across her thighs at half-mast, he slipped a hand up between her legs, nudging her thighs apart, sending his fingers to sample the moist black pussyfur and the slick cunt lips. When his probing fingers found her gaping vagina, Gloria gave out a long desperate groan, quivering, while he fingered her, testing her wetness, her heat, the promise of things to come.

Except for the tiny whimpers coming from the tantalized woman, the scene was played in eerie silence. Now, for the first time, he began to speak to her, softly, soothingly, as though to a child. In velvet tones he assured her that she had a most admirable ass, an altogether perfect ass—one just made for spanking. He laid a gentle hand on her tender bottom, letting it rest there lightly, while he described her perfectly proportioned, nicely shaped bottom as it lay before him. As he talked he placed the other hand on the shallow dip of her lower back, then pressed down, pinning her firmly in place, while her hips squirmed under his hand. He told her he intended to give her a spanking that she would never forget.

As he talked raised his hand up high watching her cowering cheeks cringe in fearful anticipation. And when he brought his flattened hand down it was with a crisp authority, delivering a glancing smack that sent her naked mounds wobbling. Gloria yelped, more surprised than hurt. Her shoulders jerked upward as her heels kicked up in back, but he held her steady, pinned in place over his lap. He watched the muscles of her buttocks clamp down, the sides hollowing out, as she steeled herself for the next crisp smack. But he held his hand, waiting for her to relax, the butt muscles to slacken, and only then did he strike again, smacking her vehemently, right across the center of the taut wobbly mounds. Gloria shrieked and kicked up her heels, but he gave her no respite, settling into a steady rhythm, spanking the girl with a cold determination, attacking her heaving bottom with quick hard smacks while she bounced and yelled, kicking her nyloned legs wildly, and squirming in fiery agitation.

A smile curled his lips as he watched his hand splatter those juddering mounds, enjoying their bouncy resiliency. For the first few smacks, Gloria tensed up, raising her head and shoulders and holding her stocking clad legs in a rigid straight line, while she tightened her cowering cheeks in anticipation of each slap. But nothing she could do would lessen the terrible agony of his methodical walloping, and soon she gave up even this feeble resistance, and lay passive, determined to endure what she must.

But even though she stoically resolved to take all he could dish out, Gloria couldn't bear this relentless spanking for long, and she was soon crying out again, this time more vehemently, begging him to stop. She yelled and cursed at him, alternately pleading with him and ordering him to stop, frantic with fiery agitation. Her nylon-sheathed legs flailed wildly. She twisted, and almost fell off his lap. But he pressed her harder with his pinioning hand, crushing her warm breasts against his hairy thighs while he renewed his attack. And after several more well-placed slaps, he sensed that the last shreds of resistance were crumbling. She yielded totally, let herself go limp, passively accepting the spanking her determined lover dished out. The resounding echoes of his hand striking the quivering mounds mingled with her sharp yelps.

When at last he finally stopped, his aching palm was tingling and he was breathing hard, uncomfortably warm and sweating from his efforts and from the electric excitement of having this naked woman squirming hotly in his lap while he walloped her vulnerable behind.

Now he studied that freshly spanked bottom, the twin mounds blazing angrily with a bright scarlet tinge. She flinched when he laid a gentle hand on her tenderized bottom, and got from the punished girl a little moan. She waited fearfully, but this time his only intention was only to let his hand rest there, lightly cupping one of those lovely, infinitely caressable rearcheeks, feeling the heat, the radiating warmth of her well-punished, womanly behind.

The long body of the black-haired girl lay like a rag doll, the sound of soft sniffling coming from her inverted head. Without warning, Decker suddenly jumped to his feet, spilling her onto the carpet. Slightly bedraggled, the stunned woman crawled up onto her elbows, and twisted around to look up at him. Her face was flushed, her eyes red and swollen. The remnants of dried tears streaked her cheeks. Decker ripped off his robe and stood naked over the sprawling figure, who gazed up at him in confusion.

"Get up," he ordered curtly.

Slowly, the tall brunette pulled herself together and rose to her full, stately height. He marveled at how she managed to keep a certain measure of dignity even though she stood before him, freshly spanked and clad in nothing but her stockings and the displaced panties which still spanned her thighs. To Decker, she looked more beautiful than ever. He closed on her and she looked up at him with eyes narrowed seductively, her lips half-parted, and her face flushed with sexual desire. Her breasts rose and fell in measured undulations, the brash nipples unashamedly erect, pertly upstanding, taut with excitement. And when he looked into her eyes he found a dewy soft look of loving surrender.

This time it was Gloria who reached out to him, and she pulled his naked body to her, clutching him tightly, feverishly kissing his neck and face and cheeks and lips, fastening on his mouth in a long, passionate kiss. Her open mouth pressed hard against his, as she squirmed lustily against his hard body, her own passions fully aroused. Decker let himself be kissed, felt his upright cock being pressed into her soft underbelly, felt the powerful urgency of the aroused woman, and sensed his own control slipping rapidly away. He grabbed her arms and disentangled himself, holding her at arm's length, staring into her excited eyes, his breath coming hard and heavy.

"Over there . . . by the couch," he managed to get out in a strangled voice. In a heated rush, she made her way to the place he pointed to, shuffling a little, still hobbled by the binding panties.

Now he placed her with her knees up against the side of the couch, bending her over the padded arm till she rested on her elbows, on the overstuffed pillows. Next, he crouched behind her, assisting her to lift each foot in turn so he could free her from the encumbering underpants. Then he nudged her ankle, urging her to widen her stance, and with one quick movement got to his feet and stepped up close behind her upturned bottom, his aching manhood throbbing with need.

The salacious picture she presented, bent over and ready for mounting, fired his lust, and with hands trembling with excitement, he grabbed her. Holding her by the hips, he maneuvered his erection up against her tight crack. He shoved his hips forward, forcing his stiffly erect prick deep between the warm heavenly pillows, snuggling it deep into the hot, moist valley, where he gave a little wiggle just to let her know he was there.

Gloria, feeling deliciously wanton at the impertinent masculine presence in that most intimate place, twitched her ass in wild excitement, and began to rhythmically clamp her butt on the rigid penis. A low hum of dreamy contentment came from deep in her throat, as he answered her excited squirmings with his own, all the while struggling to hang on to his slipping control.

When he realized he was too near the edge, Decker abruptly stepped back and, flexing his knees, guided the swollen head of his pulsing cock up between her moistening thighs, to probe the slick entrance to her cunt. With a single, vicious thrust he bucked his hips, plunging into her, to bury his prick to the hilt, so that his driving pelvis smacked against her still-smarting behind. The swiftness of his penetration took the woman's breath away, and she sucked in air through clenched teeth, as she shivered, and shook beneath him. And when his pounding hips ground solidly against her ass as he buried himself in her, she tossed back her head and groaned in an earthy growl of animal passion.

She was a woman possessed, moaning and twisting in sensual abandon, flinging her rich mane from left to right, rearing up in ecstatic delight as wave after wave of heightened pleasure wracked her writhing body.

Caught up in his own overpowering lust, Decker pumped into the raging woman, furiously hammering against her tenderized mounds, then grinding his hips against her solid meaty bottom and reigniting the simmering fires in her throbbing behind. Gloria's moan was low and plaintive. The dull pain of his pounding hips lent a piquancy to the overwhelming rush of pleasure sweeping over her.

She sensed her own climax approaching and clamped her eyes shut. Her pretty features were contorted with sexual urgency. She was grunting like an animal, making abrupt sounds through clenched teeth at each determined stab of his thrusting prick. Then she was moving with him, bucking her hips against the padded arm of the couch, matching his fucking movements with her own as she tossed and churned in erotic frenzy.

Decker heard himself groan, felt an involuntary quiver shoot through him as the excited tingling escalated wildly. Then he felt a deeper tremble begin in the woman bent beneath him, felt it ripple up her legs and shake her ass in demented fury. In seconds the trembling built to a tremendous shudder, and massive uncontrollable contractions racked her as she arched up off the couch, straining upward as powerful orgasmic thrills pierced her soul.

Gloria threw back her head in wild abandon, whimpering in a high-pitched whine, just as Decker felt the onrushing surge of his own thundering climax. A spasm of intense pleasure electrified him and sent the two of them riding the wave of a crashing orgasm, sweeping them up in a flood of pure rapture that seemed to go on and on.

CHAPTER SIX

DECKER AWOKE, vaguely aware of the sound of tinkling water coming from the bathroom. In a moment he heard the flush of the toilet, followed by the sudden rush of the roaring shower. In time Gloria emerged from bathroom, all freshly scrubbed and pink, her warm, glowing body wrapped in a fluffy towel, one end tucked between her breasts. A smaller towel, arranged as a makeshift turban, bound up her still wet hair. He lay on his back, watching her pad around the room, systematically gathering up her clothes.

"What are you doing?"

"Oh . . . good morning, lover. I'm getting dressed. Do you have a hair dryer? I'm famished. I thought we could go out and get something to e . . ."

"Come over here," he beckoned.

She came to the side of the bed, looking down on him, a quizzical expression on her face.

"Get rid of the towel."

With a shrug, she undid the tuck and let the towel slip to the floor.

"The other one, too."

The turban was undone, and the thick damp mass fell in ropy tresses, hanging down limply so the sopping wet strands lay plastered over her naked shoulders.

He sat up and swung his legs over the bed, reaching for his cigarettes. He left her standing there, without a stitch, all warm and moist and desirable. He eyed her up and down, noting the damp black curls that marked the plump wedge of her pubis. He had some things to tell her, about what he had planned for the weekend.

There was no reason to go out. They would spend their time together here, in his sprawling place overlooking the valley. There was plenty of food; she could start by making breakfast.

While he talked he got up and went to rummage through a set of dresser drawers. She watched him step into his briefs; pull on a pair of jeans and a black T-shirt. Then he reached in another drawer to toss onto the bed a handful of lingerie.

Gloria slipped into the flimsy top, a black camisole which she drew down till the thin ribbons looped her shoulders, and the short hem hung loose, barely kissing her hips. The filmy thing hung loosely on her, its generous scoop neck leaving bare much of her upper chest while the diaphanous fabric did little to conceal the seductive shape of her breasts or the thick disks of her prominent nipples, all of which were easily discernable through the smoky haze. She had to smile when she picked up the matching panties and held them up to examine them. The words *spank me* had been stenciled across the seat in bold, pink letters. Without a word, she stepped into the underpants, and pulled them into place, while Decker never took his eyes off her. She tilted her head and gave him a perky smile: Decker grinned his approval and, with a friendly smack on her "spank-me" panties, sent her padding off to the kitchen.

* * *

It was their first weekend together, a sexual marathon that left both participants drained and thoroughly exhausted by Monday morning. Equally intense weekends would follow, long, languorous hours unfolding within the confines of the private world he created for the two of them in his starkly modern home in the hills.

The ritual never varied. On Friday afternoons the drapes would be drawn over the extended bay windows, heavy black curtains that would cut them off from the outside world. From Friday till Sunday, Gloria was seldom dressed. He delighted in seeing her nude, never tired of watching the way she moved, like an artist fascinated with his model. Or he had her put on some sexy things to model for him, prancing about in her high heels and very little else, showing off for him while he snapped off a string of photos that he would later store on a disk.

Gloria was distinctly uneasy about those images. At first she demurred, but he kept insisting and, as usual, she gave in. She found that it got her hot to pose like that, in some scanty outfit: to face the camera in nothing but wine-colored tights, or topless in a pair of his jeans, or in a dreamy pose, wearing nothing but one of his shirts, open down the front. The poses got more and more provocative. Blushing furiously, she had to swallow her embarrassment, but she had to admit to herself that it was a powerful turn-on. And even though it scared her that he would keep such images of her on his computer, she couldn't deny him that, or for that matter, anything else he wanted. And the more she yielded to his kinky demands, the more he wanted. It was a wild and reckless game they played, but she was loving every minute of it, by now addicted. Gloria sometimes wondered if she was in love.

She'd sit with him, looking over his shoulder as erotic pictures of her crystallized on the computer's screen, shocking, impossible pictures, that made her feel deliciously wicked—her "dirty pictures" he called them with a laugh. He showed her what she looked like nude, from every conceivable angle, from behind and from in front, posed her with long nyloned legs sprawled open, her sex exposed like a wanton whore, or crawling on hands and knees, and peering up at the camera with a soft seductive gaze, like a big cat on the prowl.

These slide shows would make Gloria blush, and although secretly thrilled to pose for him, she would worry in her more sober moments about all those pictures. One day, he printed out a half dozen and pinned them up on the corkboard in his den. Gloria noted, with a flare of jealousy, that he had pictures of two other women there. He never mentioned them, but they smiled down at her, as though inviting her to join their ranks. She never asked about those other girls, but it sent an odd shiver though her to realize she was not the first to pose for dirty pictures, crawling across the very same carpet, smiling up at the camera with pendulous breasts dangling below.

She well remembered another time long ago when her picture had been pinned up to be admired. It was a picture of a younger Gloria Brennan, a smiling college girl, dressed in a glitzy showgirl's costume: a sleek, body-hugging maillot of gold lame, a thin strip of white posterboard looped around her neck to form a makeshift collar, to which she had affixed a black bowtie. She posed with tophat and cane, perched on a high stool, her long legs sheathed in sexy black pantyhose; one extended straight down along the side of the stool, while the other angled down, folded back so that the high heel of her sandal was hooked on the lower rung. She liked to believe that the pose made her look, at least a little, like Marlene Dietrich. A more dispassionate observer might have pointed out that, while the kid had a nice pair of legs, her smile was a little too broad, her all-American-girl good looks just a little too wholesome, to be compared to the sultry elegance of the divine Marlene.

She had been a theater major, minoring in dance, and totally committed, at age 19, to a life in the theater. A friend had taken the pictures for her as part of a portfolio she was putting together. She hoped to show the photos to Professor Keller, reasoning that if he saw how great she looked in the costume, he might be more inclined to cast her in the lead in the musical the college was doing for the season's finale. She knew that she was being considered for the starring role, but so was Rachel.

And Rachel was the only girl in the company who might take the part from her. She was also tall, almost as tall as Gloria, with high cheekbones and striking good looks. And if she didn't have Gloria's easy social graces, there was something about her air of aloof indifference that gave her a strange appeal. Rachel had been trained in ballet, and was a very good dancer. While Gloria enjoyed dancing, and worked hard at it, often putting in long hours at the rehearsal studio, she soon realized that she had started too late in life to be really proficient in that most demanding art form.

And so she took her pictures with her when she went to see Professor Keller about the play. He seemed pleased to see her. He was most interested in discussing the play with her, because, he confided, he had always thought of her as one of his most talented and insightful students. Warmly encouraged by his flattering remarks, she drew the photos out from the portfolio, offering them for his inspection.

He seemed delighted at her initiative and asked a great many questions about the photos themselves. She again brought up the play, but he seemed more interested in talking about photos, and what was necessary to put together an effective portfolio. He asked if she had any more pictures of herself, and was a little disappointed to find that she did not.

Now he suggested that that be remedied. He himself often did photographic work, he told her. Indeed, he had helped several former students put together winning portfolios. And with his extensive contacts on Broadway, he was able to see to it that those portfolios got to the right people.

Gloria was thrilled that he would take such a personal interest in her, flattered, and only too happy to have the guidance of a professional who was so familiar with the ways of the theater. And so they arranged a photo session. He had a studio and darkroom in his basement, since he, like all the best professional photographers, did all his own developing work. She could come over some evening, and in a just a few hours she would have a set of pictures she would be proud to circulate as she developed her career.

She was a little uneasy about going alone to the professor's house since she knew he was divorced, and had something of a reputation on campus. But when she got there, she was relieved to find that his basement had indeed been set up with all the paraphernalia of a photographic studio: various cameras, tripods, lighting, and screens. She was secretly pleased when he suggested she start with some shots wearing the costume from the show. It was the same costume she had borrowed for the first set of pictures, and he had taken it overnight so they would have it for her session. She ducked behind a screen and changed quickly. And when she came out from behind the screen and felt his appreciative look, it occurred to her, and not for the first time, that his interest in her might not be purely professional.

The tight-fitted costume clung to the subtle contours of her spare, athletic body like poured molten metal, its broad scoop neck exposing her girlish chest and the first hint of cleavage between her tightly constricted breasts. The high fullness of her sleek haunches were revealed by the high cut of the sides, while in back, the swooping leg-bands arched over the girl's high-set buttocks exposing pert cheeks encased in smoky nylon.

He took many pictures of her that night, constantly snapping, adjusting the camera, having her pose this way and that. And when he suggested a few "cheesecake" photos she let herself be persuaded, although she flatly refused to pose in the nude. Still, he convinced her that there was nothing wrong with posing topless, and she reluctantly agreed. She peeled off the snug maillot and posed for him in pantyhose and heels, still wearing the tophat and the ridiculous collar.

Two days later she read the cast announcement on the bulletin board and saw that she had the starring role.

Up there on that stage, under the lights, with the eyes of hundreds of people on her, Gloria felt alive as never before. And in the end, with the steady applause ringing in her ears through multiple curtain calls, she felt a sense of wild exhilaration as she strode out alone to take her solo bow. The show was a huge success, and everyone agreed her performance had "made" the show. But the biggest thrill of all was seeing her father there the closing night of the show, sitting near the front, clapping heartily for his little girl with a look of intense paternal pride on his handsome face.

* * *

Sometimes she didn't go directly to Decker's place after work, but instead they would go out to dinner before returning to his house. It was on one of those Fridays that Decker sat looking at her across the table from him, admiring the way the subdued lighting made her seem even more beautiful. The chic frock she wore, with its flimsy spaghetti straps, left bare a generous portion of her graceful neck and softly contoured shoulders as well as the creamy smoothness of her upper chest. The fine ridges of her collarbone and the subtle dip at the sternum created supple shadows that followed the seductive contours of her uplifted breasts.

They talked about those photos, and she found herself admitting to him that she was secretly pleased, posing for him like that, although, she quickly added, she worried a little about the possible repercussions. As they talked an intriguing thought began to take shape in Decker's head.

By the time they got to his place, he had the plan well formed. They had a drink and Gloria waited, slipping out of her pumps and curling up across from him in a large naugahyde chair, folding her long legs under her in an appealingly girlish gesture. The shift caused the hem of her tight dress to ride up, revealing the banded tops of her stockings. She let it stay that way, well aware of the provocative nature of the pose, and feeling warm and loved, and blissfully uncaring.

Finally, he downed the last of his drink and stood up, silently beckoning her over. She came to him eagerly, and he kissed her and then held her out at arm's length, looking at her with a peculiar gleam in his eye. Gloria was a little taken aback.

"Let me get out of these clothes?" she whispered.

"No, not yet. Wait here." And with that he was off to the bedroom. And when he came back he was bare-chested, and in his hands he held the camera, a bunch of leather straps, and several lengths of cord.

Gloria's eyes widened when she saw what he carried. She opened her lips, but nothing came out. She instantly realized what he was going to do to her and the fleeting hesitation that went through her was immediately replaced by a familiar tingling excitement. She stood there staring at the straps, fascinated. They were thick serviceable leather straps, each a foot long or so, with buckles and D-rings sewn into the leather.

Without a word, he grabbed the paralyzed girl by the wrist and pulled her around to the back of the massive chair, leading her up to it so that her thighs were pressed up against the padded back. Stepping up close to her, he whispered in her ear:

"Bend over."

She obeyed, lowering herself, folding her long body over the thickly padded back of the chair. Now, Decker busied himself securing her in place.

First, he knelt down behind her, clasping her right ankle, and looping it with one of the straps which he cinched down and buckled in place. Then he used the D-ring to attach a length of cord from which he could tether her to the metal leg of the chair.

Before he could secure her other leg, he would have to do something about the tight-fitting dress. Of course, the easiest way would have been to have her remove it, but that would spoil the effect Decker had in mind for the photos. So, instead, he knelt behind her and, clamping a hand around each calf, slid his hands up the sides of her legs, savoring the warm slippery smoothness of those nylon-sheathed columns. Slipping his hands under the narrow sheath, he shoved the silky fabric in front of his burrowing hands till the rising hem had exposed her lacy stockingtops and several inches of bare thighs. He wedged the dress up between her belly and the back of the chair, leaving it obscenely rucked up, while he attended to her other ankle. He quickly banded her left ankle and nudged her legs apart, attaching the ankle strap to the left chair leg.

Next, he went around to the front of the chair, and grabbing her by the wrists hauled her over and down, pulling her dangling arms down along the side of the chair. Gloria, tight-lipped, closed her eyes and shivered.

Once he had her wrists cuffed, he used the remaining cords to attach them to the front legs of the chair, carefully tightening the tension until her body was a taut bow bent over the back of the chair.

There was one final detail to attend to. Throughout the procedure Gloria had waited patiently, not saying a word. She had uttered not the slightest protest and, of course, he had not expected her to. So, strictly speaking, the gag was unnecessary. Yet there was a certain value in employing the ball gag which he had slipped into his pocket, and now extracted before her widening eyes. The gag would not only stifle any outbursts, but more importantly, it would further increase her growing sense of helplessness. Grinning broadly, he showed it to her, and winked, holding it up before her eyes. The hard rubber ball with the leather strap threaded through it was about the size of a tennis ball.

"Open wide," he ordered.

Gloria closed her eyes, swallowed once, and then she submissively opened her mouth to accept the hard rubber ball. He held her head and wedged the ball in between her teeth, while buckling the strap around her head, imprisoning a wad of thick hair.

When he released her head, she let it sag weakly forward. Passively limp, totally acquiescent now, Gloria felt that familiar comforting feeling of placing herself totally in the hands of her masterful lover. Now he was down on one knee just in front of her.

Her hair had fallen forward to hang down between her extended arms, partially shielding her appealing breasts which hung loosely in her sagging bodice. He was seized with a sudden desire to expose her breasts.

She never stirred as he reached up behind her and opened the little zipper at the back of the dress, and then reached inside the billowy top of the dress to scoop out those smooth wobbly mounds, freeing her breasts to let them dangle between her outstretched arms, two succulent mounds with their swollen tips of soft cocoa butter. He couldn't resist the urge to play with those sexy baubles. And so he indulged himself for a few minutes, fingering her nipples, sampling the satiny softness of those lush pendants, taking handfuls of smooth tittie-flesh, squeezing and deeply fondling those full mounds.

As he amused himself with her hanging breasts, Gloria twisted her shoulders; he heard a tiny muffled whimper come from behind the gag. It was obvious that she found this pleasant dalliance to be quite stimulating, and Decker himself felt a strong, unmistakable surge of raw lust as his rock-solid penis pressed against his pants with a surge of urgency.

Still on his knees he eagerly scuttled around behind the splayed female. Gathering up handfuls of her dress at either side, he hoisted up the slippery fabric all the way to her waist, wedging it between her midriff and the chair and folding it up in back so that it lay in neat pleats across her bent back. This pleasing arrangement exposed the entire length of her splendid legs, the smoothly contoured thighs banded by the tops of her nylons, and the rounded contours of her jutting buttocks packed into a pair of shiny peach panties.

He admired the lascivious display: This proud beauty bent in shameless offering, the nylon molded curves of her finely muscled legs rigidly planted in that widened stance, like the stems of a draftsman's compass; the sleek lines tapering down to the pointed toes of the high-heeled open sandals she still wore; and most prominently, those tautly drawn panties, thin and shiny, the waistband a delicate filigreed lace; the narrow edgings of lace repeated by the legbands. Leaning forward Decker could see that the tightly drawn gusset had become caught up in her crotch, molding her pouting cunt lips and letting a few stray pussy hairs escape on either side.

He reached for the waistband, hooking his curled fingers in at either hip to peel down those peach underpants, baring Ms. Gloria's Brennan's bottom to his insatiable gaze one more time. He never tired of the unveiling. It sent a thrill through him, to expose her like this. He left the twisted panties bunched up and spanning her thighs as he leaned forward, bringing his face close to examine those high mounded domes and the tight crack At the juncture of her thighs the bulging purse of her underslung vulva was stretched slightly by her widened stance. The soft pouch was adorned with a thicket of black pussyfur. Fine and silky, the wispy curls shaded into a little tuft that thickened between her legs.

Decker slid his hands up the curving slopes of those jutting mounds, letting them glide along the incredible silky smoothness of those tautly rounded curves. Then cupping her solid rearmounds, he gave her a friendly squeeze before quitting her ass to pick up his camera.

Now he went about the room switching on all the

lights, one after the other, till the shrouded room was ablaze in light. Gloria craned upward, watching him as he made some adjustments on his camera. The full impact of the situation struck her as he stepped behind her and began clicking away. She thought how incredibly wanton she must look: bent over and tied down, her naked bottom jutting back in lewd display, her half-masted panties stretched across her thighs, and her long legs rigid with tension, straining, as she stood poised high up on her toes. The deliciously wicked image of herself, presented in such obscene offering, thrilled her to the very core.

Meanwhile Decker snapped merrily away, taking picture after picture, crouched in front of her: a view of her heavy hanging breasts swaying from under the arched bow of her torso; from the sides, snapshots of her bending form with the disheveled dress hiked up in provocative display, the bare ass shamelessly revealed to the camera's lens; and from behind and below, sighting up between her rigid nylon-sheathed legs to the shaded crotch, probing the pendulous vagina that bulged seductively between her outstretched thighs, open and vulnerable to the camera's prying eye.

CHAPTER SEVEN

WHEN AT LAST he set the camera down, Decker got to his feet, and came around to stand directly in front of the bent-over woman, placing himself before her so she could watch him strip. First he removed his shoes and socks and then shoved his slacks down to his ankles. He took his time, carefully removing his pants and folding them neatly. Looking her right in the eye and grinning, he bent down to skim off his briefs, freeing his massive erection. Suddenly liberated, his aroused penis sprung upright in rigid attention, to stand up, quivering, just inches in front of Gloria's wide eyes. He took his swaying cock in his right hand, offered it to her, dragging the swollen head down along the side of her face. Gloria's eyelashes fluttered down at the wildly sexual thrill when his prick touched her cheek, and she found herself answering his obscene invitation, closing her eyes and straining up against that rigid penis, rubbing herself against his prick like a big cat savoring a caress with sensual pleasure.

Then, abruptly he was gone, and she opened her eyes to see him padding off to the bathroom. When Decker returned, he carried a tube of lubricant in one hand. Circling behind her tied-down figure, he studied the appealing invitation she presented: the rounded domes of her naked bottom so high-set and poised enticingly before him, the splayed legs inviting easy access to the furry underslung pussy stretched so seductively as to invite penetration.

But that particular invitation was one he meant to pass up, at least for now. For it was not her familiar cunt that he intended to visit on this particular occasion. Tonight he would explore virgin territory. Tonight, he intended to fuck the girl up the ass.

Stepping up to the bent-over woman, he placed his hands at the top of the twin contours, fitting his cupped hands to those taut mounds, molding the delicious curves of that outthrust bottom. He filled both hands with her bottom, digging his fingertips in the flesh at each side and gripping her ass firmly, relishing the smooth, hard, tautly drawn curves; the softness beneath the skin, pressing in till the softness yielded to the deep inner firmness. He massaged and kneaded those pliant asscheeks until he had the girl so hot she couldn't help responding, straining upward against her bonds, arching up neck and shoulders and emitting a series of short, staccato grunts.

He loosened his grip but let his hands linger, lovingly tracing the smiling undercurves to their nexus and beyond, letting his fingers explore the moist underarch, sampling the silky tuft of pubic hair, stroking the silken flesh of the inner thighs and following the elastic topband of a nylon before slipping a hand upward to seek the bulging ridge of her labia. He fingered the fine tendrils of black hair he found there, and pressed in hard, fondling the soft folds of her Gloria Brennan's cunt. As the tantalized woman squirmed in mounting agitation, Decker cupped her furry vulva and gave her firm, urgent squeeze. He heard an answering moan escape from behind the rubber stopper.

Now he was fingering her there, playing with the slick ridges of those distended pussy lips, while Gloria moaned with increasing desperation, tossing her head and writhing in her bonds. He noticed that her ass twitched in tiny, involuntary reactions and when he pulled his hand back, his fingers glistened with her juices, unmistakable proof of the powerful reaction his amorous play induced. She shifted from one foot to the other, unable to keep still as his teasing fingers excited her to new heights, and when he used two joined fingers to probe between the slippery folds of her cunt, Gloria whimpered in her growing frustration, and tossed her head like a magnificent mare shivering with impatience to start the race.

By now, Decker's lust had also reached a fever pitch, all his desires reduced to the single powerful urge to lay into that writhing woman, right then and there. He was tingling with sexual excitement. His pulse was racing; his palms were damp; and there was a peculiar lightness in his wrists and ankles. His prick was throbbing with the ache of desire.

He squeezed out a dollop of gel, to begin carefully greasing his erection. This time, when he reached for her, it was to splay his hands across the width of her ass, and dig his inward-pointing thumbs into the crack.

Eagerly, he pried her pliant mounds apart, revealing the tallow center strip, and a soft pink anus that winked invitingly at him. With a gob of gel on his middle finger, he poked at the puckered dimple, and got a surprisingly powerful reaction. The impertinent finger signaled his intentions clearly, and it galvanized Gloria into alarmed reaction.

Instantly, her eyes flew open, her arched eyebrows shot up, as she fully comprehended what he was about to do.

The tethered girl raised her head, straining to straighten up. With mounting distress she brayed into the gag, making sounds of helpless rage, inarticulate protests, as she shook and struggled against her restraints.

But Decker ignored her protests, and pressed on with singleminded intensity as Gloria shook her tail vigorously, her muffled protests rising in intensity. Her furious agitation only excited him more, and he quite deliberately pressed his stiffened finger into her anus.

At first, the tight ring of rubbery muscle resisted the intruder but as he persisted, applying slow steady pressure, the anus gradually yielded to him, and his finger slipped with a pop into the tightly guarded entrance. A muffled shriek came from the girl as his finger penetrated her ass. Her hips jerked forward in instinctive recoil at the abrupt violation. Gloria threw back her head and strained mightily, arching her back and craning upward. The tendons of her neck stood out in angry defiance, as she pulled against the taut cords holding her wrists; her fists clenched in helpless rage.

But Decker calmly pressed on, rimming the entrance with the lubricant, rotating his finger, screwing it into her, while the impaled woman twisted and squirmed helplessly like a fish on the hook.

Inexorably, he worked his finger all the way up her rectum, till his cupped hand was pressed firmly against the contoured roundness of her bottom, while she gurgled from behind the gag. Then deep inside her, he jiggled the intruding finger just a little, before beginning a slow extraction, fascinated by the way the tight ring sucked greedily at his withdrawing finger.

Now he set his stance, holding her straining cheeks apart with one hand while he gripped his cock with the other and guided the lust-swollen head up against the small rosette. Slowly he pressed his cock into her. Gloria's head snapped back and she tossed it furiously, flinging her loose hair in all directions as he bore in on her. She was screaming into her gag, as he forced the rear gate for the second time. She strained to clamp her buttocks while the tiny orifice resisted stoutly; but the man was not to be denied, and it suddenly gave way under his determined assault. As the crown of Tommy Decker's rigid penis slid into Gloria Brennan's anus, she shrieked into her gag, following that with a series of short staccato yells, cries of pure animal outrage. She shook her ass and worked her sphincter muscle in a vain attempt to expel the intruder, but he had gained entrance by now and was in too deep to be easily dislodged.

Slowly, inexorably, he forced his ravaging prick right up her twisting bottom. The tight-fitting sleeve gripped his penis like a small fist. And while she tossed and groaned in agony, he pressed on, not satisfied till he was buried to the hilt, his hips pressed up against the solid curves of her upturned bottom. For a moment he held himself there, letting her adjust to the novel sensation of having a prick up her ass, while he savored the exquisite feel of that incredibly tight, spasming channel.

Then he started to move. At first, he made only tiny movements, barely wiggling his hips, tickling her innards with his jiggling prick. Then he slowly withdrew, watching his rigid shaft slide out of her clinging asshole. Reflexively, the skewered female clamped her buttocks on him, as he pulled back. He grabbed her by the hips and held her as he pulled back till only the very tip was inserted in her behind, and then he let himself fall forward, thrusting into the woman in a swift, brutal lunge.

Once more she threw back her head and screamed, the gag effectively muzzling the worst of her outrage. Again he pulled back and drove into her at full length. And in this way he fucked her, with slow deep penetrating strokes, sawing in and out of her ravaged asshole and fighting to hold onto his slipping control as successive waves of pleasure racked his body. Still holding her by the hips, Decker noticed that the violated female had quieted down since the shock of the first penetration. Her agitated movements had all but ceased, till she was actually holding herself perfectly still, simply letting herself be fucked.

For Gloria, the burning sensation of having a solid cock lodged up her bottom had lessened considerably, and was now yielding to a new and different feeling. Forcing herself to relax eased the pressure, the pain lessened, and she felt his stiffness filling her, a queer sensation of being overfull, not at all unpleasant, and then there was a vague tingling sensation. A shock of illicit excitement rippled through her as she pictured herself bent over and being mounted like an animal, being shamelessly used by this powerful, lusty male.

Decker renewed his grip on her hips, his eyes closed, his jaws clenched tightly, as he struggled to hang on. Now he sensed a new movement on her part. It started as a barely perceptible trembling in her loins, then became more pronounced, more definite tremors that racked her bent body. Her hips began to move and soon her ass was wiggling in heated arousal. Then the movement in her hips became more defined, settling into a definite jogging as she thrust her impaled bottom back at him, meeting his pounding thrusts with her own.

Her excitement fired him to greater heights. He was lustily driving into her, and soon had the woman churning and bucking wildly in the grip of full-blown passion. Her sudden explosive reaction was enough to send Decker careening over the edge, and he raced to finish her off with maniacal fury, feeling the onrushing surge of plea-sure rise up in him. He hung on the brink of ecstasy for just a moment more and then he let his control melt away, and in that absolute moment of triumph, gave himself up to the sweet rapture flooding over him. An intense thrill rocketed through his body as the first powerful jet of cum erupted from his pulsating prick. Then he threw back his head and groaned, pumping into her with wild abandon, while she shook and trembled beneath him.

Gloria, thrashing about in erotic frenzy, thrust back her ass against his pelvis, seeking to impale herself even fur-ther, to capture every inch of his pulsating cock. She rel-ished the sense of fullness, the heat spreading from her bowels to her womb, the throbbing in her womb. Repeated thrills electrified her. She was on fire, greedy and eager for more of him, for more cock, more prick, more of his rutting penis up her ass. She was insatiable: a lusty woman wanting it all.

She sensed the sudden tension in his straining body, the deep throbbing of his prick, the sudden eruption in her bowels. Immediately, she was seized by her own orgasm, as an abrupt intense bolt of ecstatic delight shot through her, sending her into shattering paroxysms of pleasure. She clenched her eyes and braced herself against the overwhelming onslaught as a massive convulsion shook her. And then she was over the edge, and riding the crest of a long endless wave of pleasure. From behind the ball gag, Decker heard the sound of a low wavering moan of deep-seated satisfaction.

Gloria was slumped over, her shoulders heaving, her head lolling weakly. She barely stirred when her lover withdrew his depleted cock and dismounted. And now she stood perfectly still. He left her like that, gagged and bent over the back of the chair. He left her while he, still naked and feeling pleasantly drained, sprawled back languidly on the couch, and reached for a cigarette. He would allow himself these few leisurely moments, which he intended to spend smoking and contemplating the offered-up ass, the erotically powerful image the bending beauty presented to him.

CHAPTER EIGHT

IT WAS SEVERAL DAYS later that he showed up, quite unex-
pectedly, at the law firm. The neat young blonde manning
the desk just outside Gloria's office glanced up at the lean
guy with the arresting gray eyes. She studied him through
the oversized circles of thin-rimmed glasses which made
her inquisitive blue eyes even larger.

"May I help you?"

Decker quickly appraised the girl's trim, small-
breasted figure as she sat behind her desk composed in
her polite receptionist's manner. He liked the way she
wore her close-cropped hair: a wide swath of ash-blonde
silk falling rakishly across her brow, while the short sides
swept back around her small face—a boyish style that
enhanced her freshly scrubbed, youthful appearance.

"I'm here to see Miss Brennan," he replied, smiling
back at her.

The girl's thin lips tightened, turning down dubiously.

"Do you have an appointment?"

"No, but she'll see me. Just say it's Tommy Decker."

He watched her pick up the receiver and extend a slender finger to stab the button on the phone. With lips close to the mouthpiece she delivered the message in a low, conspiratorial voice. She listened for a moment, then looked up at him and nodded, brightening considerably.

"Take a seat, Mr. Decker. Ms. Brennan will be with you shortly," she said, dismissing him with her best receptionist's smile.

Decker nodded and glanced at his watch. He waited, but he didn't take a seat. He hated to be kept waiting . . . for anything. He would give her two minutes, no more. Somewhat to his surprise, the door opened almost immediately, and Gloria came out to meet him, smartly dressed in an expensive navy blue suit. The pale blue blouse she wore, with its ruffled front and lavender ribbon-tie, lent a nice feminine touch to the otherwise austere outfit.

She swept through the door with a slightly bewildered smile, clearly taken aback by this collision of her two worlds. With a glance at her secretary, she mumbled something to Decker about a pleasant surprise, immediately hating herself for sounding so trite. There was an awkward pause as she stood face to face with her lover in the offices of her law firm. He didn't help her out; just stood there with that little grin of his. Hastily, to hide her confusion, she ushered him into her private office, telling the blonde, a girl named Sarah, to hold all her calls.

Sarah watched the door close on the two of them, a thoughtful expression on her face. She had been Gloria Brennan's administrative assistant for two years now, and she had never seen her usually poised and confident superior so obviously flustered. She wondered, not for the first time, about Gloria Brennan's private life. With her, Gloria had always been strictly business, and she never gave Sarah the slightest hint that she even *had* a life out-side of the office.

Well, it didn't matter, she decided. Still, she couldn't help wondering about the thin man with the military bearing who moved with the ease of quiet authority even as he let himself be led into Gloria's inner office. The blonde girl shook her head in mild exasperation, as she turned back to the appointment book that lay open before her. This was sure to throw off Ms. Brennan's afternoon schedule.

Decker eyed the spacious glass-walled office apprecia-tively. Tastefully furnished, with its panoramic view of the city, it was an office designed to impress, to make a statement about the status of its occupant, and by infer-ence, the prestige of the law firm. He prowled restlessly, ignoring her offer of a chair, and circling the room, criti-cally eyeing the furnishings, as though he was consid-ering whether he wanted to buy the place. He paused in front of a teak credenza, stopping to study a set of primi-tive figurines: Three hardwood rounded cylinders of varying sizes, with their pointy heads and carved inlay features; totems of some obscure pagan gods. He picked up the taller one and examined it with idle curiosity, run-ning his hand along the smoothly polished shaft absently while he looked out the window. She watched him set the Pre-Columbian piece down and continue his inspection of her office, circling around behind her desk, and even-tually settling himself comfortably in her executive's chair. He leaned back expansively, his feet on her desk and smiled up at her.

"I just came by to say hello. Aren't you glad to see me?" he asked, smiling up at her with that innocent boyish grin she knew so well.

"Of course, darling. It's just that we're really rather busy today and I . . ."

"Come here," he beckoned.

She seemed to consider for a moment, then, with a weak smile, capitulated, stepping around her desk to the spot he pointed to beside the chair.

"I want to see what you're wearing." He smiled up at her, his eyes sparkling with impish delight.

"But, you can see. I don't . . . " she began in confusion.

"Come on now Gloria, you know what I mean. It's not that junior executive outfit of yours I want to see. It's what you have on *under* it. Come on now . . . let's take a look. Lift up your skirt!"

Gloria could scarcely believe her ears. Struck motionless, she could only stare down at the man whose grin never faltered. Her lips parted as if to say something, but nothing came out. Meanwhile, Decker's eyes met hers with perfect equanimity. He simply sat there, enjoying her distress, and smiling up at her the whole time with that wry grin—the innocent smile of his that seemed to say, *why are you making such a big deal out of this?* The man was playing with her, smug and secretly amused.

"Don't be silly, Tommy. We *can't* mess around here!" she hissed. She was clearly rattled and becoming increasingly irritated. "Not in the office!"

The smile faded from his lips, but his gaze never wavered. Those steel gray eyes held her pinned to the spot. Once more he repeated the implacable command, this time enunciating each word in a calm, cool, collected voice.

"Lift up your skirt!"

An erotic quiver knifed through her core at the lewd command. It was crazy! Unthinkable! Here, in her office? What if someone walked in! She felt a tingling of wild excitement at the recklessness of it all, and involuntarily clenched her thighs at the thrilling thought of danger.

Clearly distraught, Gloria wanted to say something. She opened her mouth, but the words wouldn't come. He held her paralyzed in his gray, unwavering stare. Decker seemed perfectly content to wait, self-contained, wrapped in the cold resolve of his iron will.

Gloria swallowed once, then apparently made up her mind. She leaned over the desk, reaching across him to get the phone. Suddenly, Decker was alarmed. Had he gone too far! For one awful moment he thought she was going to have him thrown out. But even though she was clearly rattled, there was enough of the sensible side of Gloria left to take a few precautions. She buzzed the outer office, while he held his breath.

"Sarah, *no* interruptions!" she snapped in an authoritarian manner that left no doubt she meant it.

Then she straightened up. He watched her with perfect serenity. Her tongue flickered out to rim her lips, and she managed to give him a little half-smile. And then his heart leaped with joy as he saw her move to obey. She reached down the sides of her skirt to gather up bunches of fabric and hoist up both the skirt, and the creamy colored underslip. Decker's eyes left her face to follow the unveiling of Gloria's beautiful legs, falling in love all over again with those sleekly elegant contours molded by the honey-tinted nylon of the pantyhose she wore. She paused with the hem held midway across her mouth-watering thighs.

"Higher." he said.

Gloria closed her eyes, took a deep breath, and hiked up her skirt the remaining few inches to her waist. A burning wave of embarrassment swept through her. This was silly! After all, she had just spent the entire weekend in this guy's place in her birthday suit, and yet here she was feeling acutely embarrassed to let him see her like this. The very thought of showing herself to him, here, in her office, got her instantly hot and bothered, tingling with wild, crazy excitement.

As she stood there swaying, with eyes closed, a sudden image came to her, a half-formed memory from her lost girlhood. She was at her Uncle's place in the country . . . a skinny tomboy . . . just a leggy kid with long black hair that fell straight, halfway down her back. They had gone into the fields to play—Gloria, her older cousin Jeff, and two of his friends.

It was a warm and sunny day, a glorious day for romping in those lush, grassy fields that seemed to go on forever. She saw herself gleefully running wild and free, racing over the gently rolling hills, flying at breakneck speed, the wind in her hair. They chased after her and she ran and ran until flushed and excited, she tumbled down over a knoll and let herself collapse. She rolled over and over in the tall grass till she finally came to rest in a slight hollow, panting for breath, with her cheek pressed against the warm earth.

Breathless and slightly giddy, she flattened herself in the high grass, hiding, till one of them found her and shouted for the others. Then they were on her. At first, it was just playful wrestling, but the game quickly got a little rougher; the excited boys more insistent, forcing themselves on her, overpowering her. She remembered the closeness, the smell and feel of their hard sweaty bodies pressing and rubbing against hers. Suddenly, she was rolled on her back. For a moment she was staring at the bright blue sky and then her cousin scrambled on top of her, wrestling with her, covering her with his weight. He eased back, kneeling up astride her hips, sitting on her belly and clamping her wrists with arms held up over her head, pinning her down while she yelled for him to let her up. She wriggled and squirmed in helpless agitation.

She felt hands clutching at her belt and realized, with sudden alarm, that someone was undoing her belt opening up her jeans. Before she could react, her jeans were being yanked down over her twisting loins. Gloria kicked and hollered, but they persisted, pulling the bunched jeans off, baring her flailing coltish legs.

The wiry girl was still struggling, straining up against her cousin's pinning weight, but she knew her resistance was futile. She was slowly being subdued, forced to yield to the giggling boys, to let them have their way. And now she felt a twinge of some new feeling. It was a feeling of being insanely pleased, secretly thrilled. It was a crazy, wild elation that came with the sudden realization that she had something, possessed whatever it was that drove and maddened these eager young boys. The thought scared her, yet sharpened her senses at the same time. She stopped her futile squirming, let herself go limp, waiting tensely, every fiber alert, detached and yet curious to see what would happen next.

But then, to her astonishment, as quickly as it started, the game abruptly stopped. Suddenly, Jeff, still sweating and breathing hard, got off her; her feverish attackers drew back, and once again became mere neighborhood boys. They released her, backing off, silly grins on their faces. Stunned, she lay there for moment, collecting herself, panting from the exertion, a little disheveled in her loose sweatshirt, thick white cotton socks, and sneakers, her straight and narrow legs exposed, underpants revealed to the leering boys. It must have been some inner alarm, some collective warning that kept them from going any further. The boys were laughing nervously now, taunting her about having seen her panties, giggling. The sense of menace melted away as they slipped back into the comfortable world of childhood, making it all into a kind of joke.

When Gloria thought about it later, she was mortified to think of the stories they'd tell their friends, but that curious sense of elation came back to her in a rush. She would remember it often, that feeling of secret pride that came to her now, the vague sense of wickedness, the illicit, mixed with that intense, indescribable joy at exposing herself. To this day, the memory left her tingling all over.

CHAPTER NINE

THE TOUCH OF HIS HAND on her leg brought Gloria back to reality. Through half-lidded eyes she looked down to see Decker's hand lightly stroking her inner thigh, while he brought his face to within inches of her pussy.

"Lovely, lovely," he crooned in admiration. The touch of his fingertips brushing up the outside of her thigh and sent a mellow warmth through Gloria, who swayed slightly, lightheaded with the pleasure of her lover's delicate, teasing caress. Using just the pads of his fingers, he glided along the gauzy nylon, following the ridge of the legband of her panties through the snug press of her slick pantyhose. His fingers continued along the curving elastic band, following it into the juncture between her thighs, and there he tested the inner warmth of her moistening cunt through the slick film of nylon. His cupped hand clamped her sex, and he began palming her vulva with a slow, deep rub that took Gloria's breath away. Her eyes closed, Gloria arched back with the sheer pleasure of it all, drawing in a sharp gasp of air through tightly clenched teeth. A shivering thrill ran up her spine.

She gave herself up to him, to the slow, warm hands that were roaming freely over her body, finding their way along the sinuous contours of her stockinged legs. Curling fingers curved to fit her thighs, sliding upward till they were clasping her firmly by the hips. She still held her skirt bunched up in her clenched fists, giving those marvelous hands of his full access to her nyloned haunches. His hands were on her hips, turning her around, backing her up till the backs of her thighs pressed up against the edge of the desktop. His grip tightened, and she felt herself being lifted up, easily hoisted up to be set down on the desktop, legs dangling down the front.

She eased down backward till her elbows rested on the padded desktop, suddenly feeling enervated, the hands robbing her of all her energy, all thoughts of resistance. Warmed by his adoring hands, she let herself drift, slipping into a drowsy torpor. Decker had the most marvelous hands of any lover she had ever known. And so she lay with eyes closed, luxuriating in the dreamy feel of those big masculine hands, so warm and comforting as they kept up that slow caress of her loins through her pantyhose.

Now the hands were back at her waist, the fingers curling into the waistband of her pantyhose, and Gloria felt herself being stripped, the clinging nylon being worked down her hips. She was only vaguely aware of what was happening to her. Somewhere there was a sudden quickening of alarm—*This is crazy* a little voice said—but the moment passed, drowned out by the blissful surrender she felt in placing herself totally in his hands. She let herself be shifted, raised up, so he could tug the nylon out from beneath her butt. Her pumps were taken off her feet; the elasticized pantyhose stretched down her thighs past her knees, and finally stripped off her dangling legs.

A shiver of ecstatic delight coursed through the girl, a piercing stab of pleasure, followed by a maddening tickle between her legs. Weakly, she lifted her head to look down just in time to see Decker's burrowing head bury itself between her thighs. The tickling intensified. With a wild thrill she realized her lover was lapping her sex right *through* the silken crotch of her panties! Gloria let out a long groan, rolling her head from side to side, caught up in the rising tide of lust engendered by the exquisite feel of Tommy Decker's extended, flattened tongue licking her pussy through her thin, wet panties.

Decker, his head buried between her sleek-muscled thighs, breathed in the strong fragrance of her woman-scent, savoring the slightly tangy smell, reminiscent of the sea. The lusty smell of a woman in heat drove him crazy. With his hard cock throbbing, he had no desire but to pleasure the sensuous woman using broad flat strokes, lapping the inside of her crotch till the damp gusset was plastered to her swollen cunt lips, thoroughly soaked with his saliva and her own oozing love juices. When he had her whimpering helplessly, he paused and pulled back so that he could reach up and peel down her panties. The buff-colored underpants momentarily got caught up in the sticky wetness of her damp cleft. He tugged them free, and yanked them down to her ankles and off entirely, and Gloria felt marvelously free. She didn't notice that he casually pocketed her moistly fragrant underpants.

But even had she seen him steal her underwear, she wouldn't have cared. For by now, Gloria was beyond caring, only vaguely aware of what was happening to her.

Once more the little voice in her brain whispered its warning, but she couldn't hold onto the message. The passion-soaked girl was helpless, her mind a blank, as she gave herself up to the rolling waves of mindless pleasure, twisting and turning languidly while she was stripped of her underwear. Now he nudged apart her loose legs and clamped a hand on her opened crotch, fondling the slick folds of her pussy lips, massaging the fleshy softness of her naked sex through the thick profusion of tiny curls, using his thumb to tease her clitoris, firing her lusty arousal to dizzying heights while the distracted woman tossed and moaned softly, biting her lip to keep from crying out.

Then, suddenly, he was gone; those dreamy, pleasuring hands had abandoned her burning body. Bewildered, and a little groggy, she raised herself up further just in time to see her lover advancing on her with the long pointed figurine held purposely in his right hand. She gave out a tiny *oh*, and her eyes widened as he stepped up between her legs and reached down to fiddle with her cunt lips, prying the fleshy gates back with his splayed fingers while he inserting the makeshift dildo into her hot, throbbing, needy cunt.

Gloria threw back her hair and groaned at the breathtaking suddenness of the swift penetration. He soon had her writhing in frantic urgency as, grimly determined, he smoothly shoved the smiling idol right up her gaping vagina. Gloria's knees rose up, instinctively welcoming the penetration, steepling back till her knees were practically touching her breasts as her determined lover drove the teakwood shaft up right her cunt. She flung her head about, mumbling incoherently, as he pressed the wooden phallus all the way home, stuffing her distended cunt with the perverse dildo. Then he grabbed the flaring base and twisted it, screwing it into her while Gloria gurgled from deep in her throat. She shut her eyes tightly, her face contorted, her jaws clenched, as she arched back on the desk, her heels kicking wildly in the air. Suddenly, he was fucking her with the makeshift dildo, gripping the base and pumping his fist in short choppy strokes. Laying back on her elbows, head tossed back, teeth clenched, Gloria uttered tiny grunts punctuating each thrust of the grinning idol.

Her escalating passion inflamed Decker's simmering lust. Wildly excited by watching the beautiful woman's sensual squirming, and hearing the soft moans of pleasure she was now making, he pumped even more furiously, driving the frenzied, dark-haired girl to even greater heights of ecstasy. Soon he had her whimpering, emitting a high-pitched keening sound as she sensed the imminent approach of her onrushing climax. She was gyrating wildly now, totally out of control, thrashing about on the desktop, and snapping her head from side to side, while her legs flailed the air.

Abruptly, she raised her hips high off the desk, bucking up to meet his pistoning fist and she gave out a long, desperate moan. Then her body stiffened and she hit the peak of a massive orgasm. At that precise moment Decker shoved the smoothly-polished shaft in all the way and left it there, while the impaled woman trembled and shook before finally collapsing back onto the desk with a deep soulful sigh, her arms outstretched, sprawled legs dangling over the edge.

Decker dropped backward into the large leather chair, fascinated by the way the tendons along her inner thighs spasmed in tiny aftershocks. He left it in her, and the idol still protruded from the slightly mounded bulge of her furry pussy, distending the swollen, dark pink lips with its obscene bulk. The thick mat of black pubic hair around the flattered base was soaked with her love juices. Gloria lay exhausted, her bare bottom on the padded desktop, her skirt bunched up around her waist, her labored breathing gradually subsiding, the only sound to be heard in the stillness of that room.

When he extracted the idol, she stirred and gave a little *oh,* but that was all. The wooden phallus was sticky, still glistening with the residue of her copious juices. He put the grinning idol back in place alongside its two smaller brothers on the credenza, and settled back in the big executive chair, prepared to wait for Gloria to come down to earth.

In a few moments she stirred. He helped the dazed woman to her feet. Mindlessly, she bent over to retrieve her shoes and pantyhose, and it was then she realized she couldn't find her panties. Decker informed her that he wanted a souvenir of the occasion. She managed a weak smile. *Nothing* this raunchy guy did could surprise her anymore!

Shrugging, she sat her bare bottom on the desk. He watched as she drew on her pantyhose, tugging them into place up around her hips, shoving her stockinged feet back into her pumps. Next, she reached up under the twisted skirt to straighten her slip and pull the skirt back into place, smoothing it out, and tucking in her disheveled blouse. Finally, she pulled a mirror out of her desk and greeted her mussed-up image with an exasperated sigh. She hunted for a brush and comb and with brisk, efficient strokes soon straightened her hair, and then went on to carefully repair the damage to her makeup. It was while she was engaged in the ritual gesture of applying her lipstick that he asked her about her young assistant.

He learned that her name was Sarah McChesney, and she was in her mid-twenties. Somewhat reluctantly, in response to his insistent probing, Gloria told him what she knew about Sarah's life outside the office. His sudden interest in the young girl was obvious, and Gloria felt a pang of jealousy. He wanted to know all about her. But Gloria knew very little about the girl's private life. She had come to the firm right from college; an English major, from some Ivy League school—Brown, Gloria thought. She was one of those quietly competent girls, always neatly dressed, a quick learner. An efficient worker, but one who viewed her job as a sort of way station, something to do while she waited to see what life might offer her. Office rumors had it that she had a live-in boyfriend, some college kid who apparently was a graduate student somewhere. But Gloria had heard the other girls talking, and it seemed there was a recent split-up—one that Sarah had not taken very well. In any case, in response to Decker's question, she told him that young Sarah was now unattached—as least as far as she could tell.

Gloria didn't like where this was leading, not at all! With lipstick in hand, she drew a neat arch along her upper lip, concentrating on her image in the glass. She had, of course, noticed the way Decker had eyed Sarah in the outer office. And she had to admit, that look was understandable. Sarah was young and attractive. Damn good looking. And there were always guys hanging around her desk for one reason or another, office hangers-on who seemed always to find some excuse to be near her.

She opened an eyebrow pencil and began touching up a high-sweeping arc. Now Decker was off on a different track. He wanted to know if she ever saw the girl socially? . . . office parties . . . stopped some place after work? . . . or had her over for drinks? No, Gloria replied carefully, Sarah had been to her place only once, and then just briefly, merely to stop by to drop off some papers, Gloria explained, her suspicions deepening. She didn't like where this was going . . . at all!

But then he gave her a big smile, called her to him, and plunked her down on his lap. He reached up to cup her neck and drew her lips to his to give her a soft lingering kiss. Then told her what he had in mind. Gloria thought he was crazy, and told him so. She wanted no part of it! But he smiled at her, with the sort of bemused tolerance one reserved for obstinate children.

He ran a hand up her leg, brushing back her skirt and letting it rest, possessively, on her warm, smooth thigh. And he slowly, absently stroked the splendid length of that nylon-encased thigh as he explained to her how it might be done.

In that soft, mesmerizing tone he sometimes used during those more mellow interludes after they made love and the intense hardness of their passion had been dissipated, he spoke of love, and beauty, and the need for openness to life and all it had to offer. He flattered her, telling her she was an adventurous, passionate, highly sexed woman, one who should be willing to try new things.

He spoke calmly, but with a soft urgency underlying his words. And Gloria allowed herself to be persuaded, just as she had so many times before, yielding to his velvet, but implacable orders. As she sat there being cuddled in his lap, she felt warm and loved and terribly receptive, willing to do whatever he wanted simply because she was so eager, childishly eager to please the man. Then too, the thought of what he was proposing stirred something deep in her, made her feel all soft and mushy inside.

She well knew that his crazy idea—the two of them having sex with young Sarah was fraught with danger, might well be a serious, potentially disastrous mistake for her to make. His risk would be trifling, but for her the consequences were career-ending. Still, she allowed herself to be half-convinced that somehow, he could bring it off. There were ways of handling these things, he purred. It could be done very discreetly, he assured her with quiet confidence, and she believed him, instinctively trusting his self-assured worldliness to deal with a situation that seemed inconceivable to her. After all, so many things she had done these last few months would have been inconceivable to her just a short time ago. Perhaps he was right; perhaps the thing could be done.

And there was something about the idea, something intriguing. She had to admit she found Sarah to be an attractive girl, caught herself watching the girl move, admiring those nice legs, and the spare lines of her slim, small-breasted figure. For some reason, the thought of the young blonde writhing in the throes of sexual arousal caused vague tinglings of renewed excitement in Gloria's still-damp pussy.

And so Gloria, with terrible misgivings and great reluctance, finally let herself be persuaded. He beamed. Kissed her in warm gratitude. She had pleased her man, and that made her happy.

CHAPTER TEN

GLORIA WAS ON EDGE, vaguely put out, and irritable. In addition to being uneasy about Decker's crazy idea, she felt guilty about taking the day off. She had things to do at work, but he persuaded her to call in sick. They spent the morning making love. Normally, she might have enjoyed this illicit interlude, but today she was unusually tense, sick with worry about what she was getting herself into.

It was a little after 10:00 when he had her set the wheels in motion by calling the office to tell Sarah that she wanted to do some work at home; she hoped it wouldn't be too much trouble for her to bring over some files Gloria needed to look over.

Sarah, always helpful, assured her that it would be no trouble at all, and that she could be at Gloria's in an hour or so. Gloria specified the papers she wanted, going into more detail than was necessary, then thanked her assistant politely, and it was done!

Now, as she anxiously awaited Sarah's arrival, Gloria's

doubts began to gnaw at her. Decker had been vague about how he actually planned to manage things, but when she hung up the phone and started to get dressed, he stopped her abruptly. Wrapping himself in a large terry-cloth robe, he handed her a silk kimono. Her eyes questioned him, and she started to say something, but he smiled and nodded his silent encouragement. Now feeling decidedly uneasy, she slipped on the thin wrapper, a long jacket of metallic bronze that, when loosely belted at the waist, layered the tops of her thighs. Thus fetchingly clad, Gloria took her misgivings with her as he sent her padding off to make the morning coffee.

The sound of the doorbell startled Gloria, sending a wave of panic sweeping over her. She turned to Decker with stricken eyes, hoping for a last-minute reprieve. But he seemed oblivious to her distress. Nonchalantly, he set his cup down on the table, gave her a reassuring smile, and calmly nodded. And so with nothing but this thin satiny top to cover her nakedness, a very nervous Gloria Brennan was sent off to answer the door.

Sarah, clutching a set of files to her breast, and having prepared herself to ask solicitously about Gloria's health, was shocked when the door flew open and she was greeted by the sight of her well-built boss sexily clad in the thin kimono. The long vee of the open front was an blatant invitation to appreciate those lovely seductive breasts, and the high-riding hem left bare almost the entire length of Gloria's long and shapely legs—those gorgeous legs that Sarah had often admired.

Struck speechless, the young blonde could only stare, her blue eyes widening behind the glass disks as she took in the astonishing sight. Gloria saw the shocked disbelief in that wide-eyed gaze, yet also noted the look of honest appreciation in the younger woman's eyes as they swept over Gloria's body, and she blushed deeply.

Turning to hide her embarrassment, she ushered the bewildered girl in, hastily explaining that she wasn't really sick, but had merely felt the need to take some time off. Sarah mumbled something in reply, and Gloria went on, talking nervously, as she led her wondering assistant through the rooms and out onto the deck at the back of the house. And there Sarah encountered her second shock of the morning, for sitting behind a small circular table was Thomas Decker, a coffee cup in hand, wearing a robe, bare legs outstretched expansively. He seemed relaxed and quite at home as he sat in the sunshine, surveying the spacious lawn and the pool far below.

Suddenly the full impact of it all hit Sarah. She felt ill-at-ease, an outsider who had blundered in on a scene of domestic bliss. She smiled a nervous greeting at Decker, and stuck out the handful of files toward Gloria, eager to be relieved of her burden so she could get out of there! But Decker insisted she join them, offered her a seat while Gloria poured her a cup of coffee, both of them quite gracious and politely ignoring her feeble protests. She lingered, unsure what to do, terribly self-conscious under the man's calculating gaze.

He admired the spare lines of Sarah's lithe girlish figure: the narrow shoulders, the modest flare of her slight hips, her slim legs. Sarah was dressed traditionally in a white blouse and charcoal-gray skirt, worn with a dark blue blazer. Plain black pumps and honeyed nylons completed her smartly preppy outfit. All the while as she stood there uncertainly, she felt Decker's eyes on her. Reluctantly, she took a seat beside Gloria.

Gloria now took the lead. Sarah could tell her boss was also ill-at-ease. She was chatting nervously, making office small talk, mostly gossip, while the silent man sat there watching the two women, looking slightly amused, occasionally interjecting a comment, but generally content to let

Gloria carry the conversation. Sarah felt his eyes on her; knew he was watching her, critically appraising her, admiring the way her short, silvery-blond hair cropped up high off the back of her neck, gave her a neat, slightly boyish appearance. She glanced up to see him staring at her, and when their eyes met, she looked down and reddened visibly.

Sarah struggled bravely to keep up her end of the dialogue, all the while devoutly wishing she could make a quick retreat. Flustered, she didn't know where to look next. She alternately tried to avoid the loosely open front of Gloria's jacket and Decker's penetrating gaze, and so she kept her eyes on the table. And now out of the corner of her eye she saw Decker drop a hand down to rest it, with a proprietary air, squarely on Gloria's naked thigh.

As Gloria chatted away, the hand began to move, first describing little circles on the top of her thigh, and then slowly, inch by inch, sliding upward, till the fingers nosed under the bottom of the silken jacket to find the very top of Gloria's leg. As she nervously sipped her coffee, Sarah, trying not to look, saw that hand slip under the kimono. Gloria sat bolt upright at the sudden sally of that exploring hand; she straightened her shoulders just a little, but otherwise she gave no sign that might acknowledge that bold, yet surreptitious caress. Somehow, she managed a bright smile and grew more talkative, although what she was saying wasn't making very much sense. There was a slight, almost imperceptible change in the pitch of her voice when the impertinent hand burrowed down between her tightly pressed thighs.

All the while this game was going on under the table, Decker kept his eyes on Sarah's face. She could feel his eyes studying her intently, and that only increased her discomfort. Hurriedly, she gulped down the last of her coffee and abruptly shot to her feet, announcing that she had to get back to the office.

But Gloria stopped her once more. No, she must stay a while, another hour or so wouldn't matter. It was almost lunchtime. They were going out to eat. Perhaps Sarah could join them? They could take the papers with them. There were some things she might need to check with her. And in that manner, she continued chatting, while Sarah demurred, until Gloria overrode all of her weak protests. In that old peremptory tone that Sarah knew so well, Gloria insisted that Sarah accompany them to the restaurant. By now, Gloria had regained a measure of self-control, and she seemed like her old self, very much in charge once again.

Sarah, once she was on her feet, could no longer see what was happening under the table, but she did notice that Decker's arm had stopped moving. The pause had given Gloria time to collect herself.

And so Sarah yielded and sat down once again at the table, this time sitting with knees pressed together on the very edge of her chair, while she waited tensely to see what would happen next.

But the two of them seemed in no hurry for lunch. Decker stretched leisurely, and reached over with his left to hand to refill their cups, while his right hand began its under-the-table movements once again.

This time the reaction was almost immediate as Gloria's demeanor showed the first signs of obvious distress. Clearly flustered, her speech faltered, interrupted mid-sentence by a quick involuntary gasp, a sharp intake of breath as the pleasuring fingers crept between her legs to find her moistening sex. Suddenly, all conversation stopped. Gloria arched up and her long lashes fluttered as her lover shamelessly fondled her sex right in front of her subordinate. She closed her eyes and took a deep breath, struggling to collect herself. Then she turned to her tormentor and managed an embarrassed smile. In strangled voice she hissed:

"Tommy! Ple . . . ase!"

His eyebrows arched up. He seemed to consider, then smiled back at her.

"Okay. Let's go," he said agreed amiably, pulling back the wicked hand.

Throughout this episode, Sarah sat paralyzed on the edge of her chair, watching in wide-eyed amazement while her boss was being pleasured right before her very eyes! Now, the words that indicated an end to their little game magically released her, and she sprang to her feet.

"No!" Gloria stopped her.

Sarah stood rooted to the spot, looking down at her boss, vacillating in her confusion.

"You can't leave yet," Gloria began in a desperate rush, reaching out to grab her assistant by the arm. She quickly caught herself from her rash actions, and smiled in what was meant to be reassurance. "Please, Sarah . . . have another cup of coffee. While you're waiting, you can go over the budget figures on the Kohler case. We'll only be a few minutes."

Gloria looked up expectantly at her rattled assistant, and Sarah saw something in that meaningful look. It had a pleading quality, as though she were begging for the younger girl's help. Immobilized by the searching eyes, Sarah could think of no way out, and so she dumbly nodded her acquiescence.

She watched the two of them go back into the house through the open glass doors, and felt a little weak in the knees. As she took a seat at the table and reached for the spreadsheet, she noticed her hands were shaking. She felt unhinged, vaguely disconcerted, yet unmistakably excited by the bizarre situation.

She felt the acute embarrassment of the outsider, an interloper who had barged in on two lovers in the middle of their intimate tryst. But that wasn't right. Gloria had made a point of inviting her over, greeted her only half-dressed, and then insisted that she stay throughout the sex play that went on under the table. She was aware of the air of barely restrained eroticism, that sexual electricity that passed between the two lovers, and she shivered at the thought.

Now, she felt uncomfortably warm and, running a hand over her brow, found she was actually flushed. She was sitting in the chair just vacated by Gloria. Without thinking, she slipped a hand down between her legs, touching her pussy through the wool skirt while she clamped her thighs on her hand. Instantly, a delicious twinge of pleasure shot through her.

Alarmed, she jerked her hand back as if she had been burned. What was she doing? This was silly. She had work to do, she reminded herself sternly. Adjusting her glasses, she bent down to examine the figures. But she only found herself gazing blankly at the data in front of her; it was hopeless. She simply couldn't concentrate; the neat row of figures made no sense to her.

And so she gave up, shuffling the papers back into their folders. She was about to gather up the file when she heard the hiss of a desperate whisper coming from one of the rooms just off the hallway. Gloria seemed to arguing with the man about something; she heard the masculine reply, low and rumbling. She couldn't quite make out what he was saying and strained to listen alertly, her head cocked to one side. Then came his unmistakable groan, an animal groan of helpless passion, and she knew without a doubt—they were making love! The two of them were going at it, fucking, not more than a hundred feet from where she sat!

Instinctively, she turned in the direction of the sounds. As she peered into the shadowy interior, she distinctly heard a second groan, longer and deeper. The sound came from one of the rooms just off the hallway.

Intrigued, Sarah sat bolt upright, every sense alert; a crazy idea flashed into her head. For a brief second she struggled with inner doubts, then, on an impulse, she reached down to slip off her heels. Fired with an intense curiosity she could not contain, she jumped up and was through the glass doors, and moving stealthily on rapid, stockinged feet toward the sounds of love. She was just a few feet down the hall when she saw the half-opened door. She had the weird feeling it was like an invitation.

This whole thing was insane, and she knew it! Yet the girl couldn't help herself. She was being inexorably drawn to the hidden possibilities behind that partially opened door. Hardly daring to breathe, she crept closer to the doorway, being careful to keep well back from the opening, leaning over just enough to peer around the doorframe.

Decker was sprawled out languidly in a low-backed easy chair, his robe undone, and the side flaps brushed back to reveal his naked thighs, his hairy crotch, and a proudly upstanding erection that riveted Sarah's attention. And on her knees, between the man's splayed legs, Gloria Brennan sat back on her heels, looking up at him, her face poised just inches from his rigid penis.

Sarah watched fascinated as Gloria reached up to clasp his penis in both hands. Almost reverently, those long elegant hands explored the swollen shaft, feeling the length of his naked prick, while Decker tossed and twisted. With loving care she worked him over, one hand easing down to cradle the wrinkled sac of his furry balls while the other clutched his straining cock in a loose fist. Her grip tightened and she began to pump her fist up and down, yanking in slow steady strokes, jacking him off. Repeated thrills of exquisite pleasure rocketed through the helpless man, who arched up and gave out with another one of those low animal growls she had heard.

Gloria muttered something, and smiled up at him with

a lewd sexy grin. Then she leaned forward, bringing her mouth close, to plant a single, wet, enfolding kiss on the sensitive flesh just below the ridge of the taut crown. Wrapping slender fingers around the base of his prick, she tilted it toward her lips to favor his throbbing sex with delicate fluttery kisses, while the captive man squirmed and writhed in sweet agony.

Quickly changing tactics, Gloria gave her lover no respite from her pleasuring mouth, for now she was generously licking his upstanding cock, sending ragged paroxysms of ecstasy pulsing through his pleasure-wracked body. With broad, lapping strokes, her loving tongue ceaselessly caressed his hard, stiffened penis, till the shaft was thoroughly coated, left wet and gleaming with her saliva. Then she ducked her head to nuzzle at the underside, burrowing in between his legs to get to the hairy scrotum, which she also licked avidly.

Sarah, dumfounded, stared wide-eyed, totally absorbed in the gripping, erotic scene unfolding before her. Gloria was now working her way back to the crown, and there she paused, glancing up at him from under her long curving eyelashes, before tilting the shaft back to capture the swollen head in her pursed mouth. Forming her lips into a ring that tightened on the shaft, the elegant brunette went down on Tommy Decker, her black-haired head bobbing rhythmically: Gloria Brennan—the happy cocksucker! Decker's hands came down to cradle her head, softly guiding its pistoning movements. He threw back his head and gave out a long, satisfied sigh.

A tiny sigh escaped Sarah's lips; she slouched against the doorway for support. Without realizing it, she found she was comforting herself with a hand that had slipped up under her blazer and was now fondling her small left breast through her blouse, while she took in the riveting action through slitted eyes.

Gloria, her lovely lips draw into a taut circle, had her mouth stuffed with cock. She moved in changing rhythms, skillfully teasing Decker to the very edge of climax. She seemed to know instinctively how much pleasure the man could tolerate, when to escalate and when to retreat. Her cheeks hollowed as she sucked him off, looking up at him from beneath her long silky lashes, watching his face for each subtle reaction, playing his instrument like a virtuoso. She soon had her man groaning weakly, tossing his head from side to side as she drove him on with unrelenting waves of pleasure.

Though his hands played in her glorious hair, Decker did nothing to actively guide his lover through her task. He was quite content to lay back, and let her take the lead. He had not been surprised when he first discovered that Gloria had little experience in oral sex. But he had persisted in what he wanted, and in time she passed from tolerating his demands, to grudging acceptance, gradually coming to a genuine enthusiasm for the sport. She had, he assured her, natural proclivities in that direction. Now a single jolt of intense pleasure welled up in him as she enveloped his straining prick in her mouth and renewed her efforts, vacuuming him with enthusiastic abandon; bringing her lively tongue into play to thrill him to ever-newer heights of ecstatic delight.

His fingers dug into her thick mass of wonderful hair, luxuriating in the richness of those soft silky waves. He let out a long shivering moan as he tightened his grip on her, clamping his hands to the sides of her face to assume control of her, guiding her through the last precious seconds. Sensing his need, Gloria froze, letting him hold her head steady while he fucked her beautiful face, his hips bucking up and down frantically until he felt the churning waves of unrelenting pleasure escalating wildly, and arched up to hold his loins high in the air.

For a few inconceivable seconds, she held him on the pinnacle of a volcanic explosion, then a shattering climax crashed over him, sent him skidding down with a brilliant flash of pure unalloyed pleasure. At the first jet of sperm to erupt from his throbbing prick, he abruptly withdrew, taking aim at Gloria's flushed face. Gobs of cum spurted forth, splattering Gloria's pretty features: her forehead, cheeks, mouth, and chin. He grabbed the shaft and guided the head of pulsating his prick, decorating her elegant features with ropy globules of his thick cream. Through it all the woman stayed perfectly still, closing her eyes in mute acceptance of the cum that splattered her brow and dribbled down her closed eyelids till her cheeks were redolent with sperm, mouth and chin glistening with masculine spendings like a sticky spiderweb.

Gloria waited motionless, submissive, as the last few drops dribbled from the softening cock. The she deliberately turned toward the doorway, opening her eyes to encounter the wide-eyed astonishment of her young assistant.

Sarah was held petrified, caught in the act of heart-pounding voyeurism, her hand frozen in place inside her jacket. For what seemed to be an eternity, the two women locked eyes, and Sarah, mesmerized by the sight of that cum-splattered face and those dark sensual eyes, felt herself unable to move.

Then, she was fleeing, scrambling for her shoes and running through the house, her heart racing in a frantic effort to get out of the front door. She heard Gloria call out as the door slammed shut behind her, but she never looked back.

CHAPTER ELEVEN

GLORIA WAS FRANTIC with worry as she drove to work the next day. Rushing into the office, she learned that Sarah had called in sick. It was day of pure hell for Gloria, and, although Decker tried to reassure her, she grew even more frightened as the day wore on. By the following day, Gloria was a nervous wreck. But when she walked in the office that morning she was relieved, if only a little, to find Sarah at her desk as usual. Except for a marked coolness, the younger girl acted as though nothing unusual had happened between them. Gloria, for her part, tried to assume her familiar businesslike role: once more the crisp, confident boss with her dutiful subordinate. But it was hard to carry off. They both knew things had changed between them. And now there was something unspoken that hung in the air, like unfinished business. Both women sensed it; neither knew quite what to do about it.

Gloria worked to keep up the proper facade, but it was

eating away at her. It was impossible to meet Sarah's steady blue eyes. Inside, she was worried sick. By now, the full impact of what she had done came home to her! Sarah had always been discreet and trustworthy, a model employee. But she had never been tested in such a crazy manner before. The older woman was terrified as to what the girl might do. Thoughts of blackmail raced through her head—just one of the many repercussions of the rash act she had let herself be talked into. The humiliation would be unbearable. She would have to resign in disgrace, a scandal that the other partners would try to hush up, but without very much success. It would be the end to her career. She bitterly resented Decker for talking her into the harebrained business, and she hated herself for going along with him, knowing full well that it would end in disaster.

She should never have allowed it, *would* never have allowed it had she known the details of what he planned. But he had told her only that he wanted Sarah to see them engaged in a little light lovemaking. They might be caught in some compromising position, he explained, in the bedroom, kissing and caressing. What he was interested in, he explained, was Sarah's reaction.

She became uneasy when she realized he wanted her to greet their guest wearing nothing but the thin revealing kimono to cover her naked body. But it was only when they got to the small bedroom that she realized what he had in mind. Before she had a chance to react, he had grabbed her, pulled her to him and kissed her hard; when he released her, he held her at arm's length for a moment, looking her squarely in the eye. Then, he clamped his hands firmly on her shoulders and silently forced her down to her knees. Helplessly, Gloria felt her knees weaken; she sank under the steady pressure. Panicking, she hissed her vehement refusal, terrified that the girl might hear them.

She shook her head. It was unthinkable for Sarah to see her like this, on her knees, sucking a man's cock! But that was exactly what Decker had in mind. In fact, she now fully realized, he had had it in mind all along! He cut short her whispered protests, muttering something about what a beautiful cocksucker she was as he released her, and paused to run a loving hand over her cheek. Gloria mumbled her *nos*, more of an entreaty now than angry refusal, but Decker noted to his immense satisfaction, that when he released the pressure on her shoulders, she stayed put, on her knees before him. Now, he stepped back and collapsed into the big, rounded, leather chair, throwing open his robe and spreading his knees in obscene invitation. Extending one finger, he silently beckoned her to him. And Gloria, caught once more in that powerful will he possessed, did as she was told, shuffling forward on her knees to the spot that he pointed to, right between his opened knees. She edged closer till his naked erection stood just inches from her face.

He looked down on his woman, inordinately pleased to see the exquisite, black-haired beauty submissively take her place on her knees before him. He reached down to undo the loosely belted kimono, flipping it open so that he could better appreciate the flattened cones of her gently mounded breasts. He couldn't resist reaching down to finger her right nipple, lightly pinching and tugging that crinkly bud between thumb and forefinger.

Gloria gasped, sucking in a hiss of breath through clenched teeth. She closed her eyes and the erotic image that Sarah would see flashed through her mind: Ms. Brennan, on her knees, wearing nothing but the open kimono on her shoulders, her breasts jiggling, swaying heavily under her as she leaning forward to pleasure the sprawling man whose powerful, gorgeous cock stood waiting to accept her obsequious devotion.

The deliciously wicked thought sent a surge of arousal through her, a thrill of intense excitement that raced up her spine and caused her shoulders to quiver. She gave herself up to the sensations of wild abandon that threatened to overwhelm her, yielding to them, letting her inhibitions melt away, feeling marvelously free and incredibly wanton and uncaring. She wanted him, and even as she reached for his stiffened manhood, she sensed the witnessing presence standing in the doorway.

And when the act was done, and she turned her cum-splattered face toward the girl in the doorway, she found herself staring into those penetrating blue eyes, eyes filled with shocked disbelief, eyes that captured hers and were frozen there—unable to move. For a moment that seemed like eternity, the two women just stared at each other, and the other woman's knowing look thrilled Gloria like she had never been thrilled before. A sensation of the most exquisite, perverse pleasure rippled through her and caused her to shiver with excruciating delight.

Even now when she thought about it, it filled her with excitement; her thighs clenched under her desk as she tried to recapture the delectable receding traces of that singular thrill.

But the thought of that moment also brought on the sense of dread. She closed her eyes at the familiar sickening feeling in her stomach. What had she done?

Now she found that she was trying to avoid Sarah whenever possible. She went out of her way to avoid being alone with her assistant, and Sarah, for her part, seemed to be doing the same thing, avoiding direct confrontation, sending e-mails where she might once have simply walked in to ask for instructions.

And so that long week passed with only minimal contact between the two women. The days passed, but the tension didn't subside, and it was with a great deal of relief that Gloria finally greeted the weekend.

Weekends with Decker had fallen into a now-familiar pattern. She would arrive after work, her small overnight case in hand to be welcomed into the darkened interior of Decker's house, the door would lock behind her with a click of finality. The blinds would have already been drawn, the windows heavily draped, so that no sliver of the outside world could intrude. The rooms were dimly lit, kept that way for the entire weekend, unless he intended to use his digital camera. For three days there would be no distractions: no cellphones, no newspaper, TV or radio; no news of the outside world. Thus isolated, their world would be reduced to the confines of that house.

It always amazed Gloria that, from the moment she first stepped into that darkened cloister and heard the sound of the lock sliding into place, the world she left behind ceased to exist. And Gloria Brennan, the person she had worked so hard to create, the hardened, intelligent, competent attorney, evaporated to leave herself adrift and rudderless, her sense of purpose and self-centered drive yielding so easily to Tommy Decker's soft persuasive tones, velvety tones that overlay that iron will.

She felt wanted; safe and warm with Decker, secure in his place. She gave herself to this man, became his woman, his kept woman, a naked love slave kept captive in those plush surroundings for drifting hours on end. The clocks had disappeared. He made her surrender her watch at the door. Gloria lost all track of time; days and nights ran together in alternating sessions of leisurely and powerfully intense lovemaking.

In the hothouse atmosphere, with its air of unrelenting sensuality, she discovered a deeper level of intimacy than she had ever known with any man before. She had no secrets from him. All notions of personal privacy were made irrelevant. He insisted she leave the door open when she went to the toilet—Smiled at her as she sat peeing on the toilet. He'd walk in on her while she was in the bathtub, and he stay to watch, sitting on the john and supervising every detail of her ablutions.

Gloria was intrigued to find that a part of her could actually stand back and watch what was happening to her. She knew what was happening, and she let it happen. For once she accepted his quiet domination; it was so much easier to drift along, actually rather pleasant to allow things to flow in the course he determined. She found a certain inner peace, contentment in that total surrender, a feeling she had never known before.

And then there were his friends. She soon found that Decker had a close circle of like-minded people, mostly young and middle aged professionals, many of them couples, swingers who tended to gather periodically for quiet evenings, sometimes at his place, get-togethers that included shared, and sometimes very unconventional, sexual experiences. Gradually, he introduced Gloria to this little group of friends, and a new way of life began to open up to her.

Soon Gloria was totally immersed in this double life; it was all wickedly illicit, kinky and strangely, wildly exciting. She was exhilarated by the danger of being unmasked, thrilled by the sheer audacity of the secret life the two of them shared, alone. That is, until now. She simply had to talk to him about this thing with Sarah!

But when she saw him that Friday afternoon, he would not hear of it. They would discuss it later, he told her with his usual quiet authority. And so it was not until the next day that she had an opportunity to bring up the subject that was very much on her mind.

They had just returned from a rare venture outside, something he seemed to want to do more often of late. It had been a warm and sunny day, a perfect day for being outdoors, and he had announced they were going for a walk. He had been taking pictures of her in a white camisole, a short satiny thing with wispy shoulder straps, a wide scoop-neck, and a low-cut neckline edged in delicate lacy scallops. He liked the way she looked in that, and saw no reason for her to change. She could simply slip a blouse on over it; the crepe see-through would do nicely. With that, he suggested, a pair of abbreviated denim shorts; no need for panties. Finally, he had her step into a pair of high-heeled sandals and stand in front of the mirror, so she could see what she looked like in the audacious outfit.

Gloria had to admit, as she appraised her tall slender form so provocatively clad, that the image that stared back at her looked damn good. She was pleased with her breasts, medium sized, nicely respectable breasts which, braless, were slung a little low on her long torso, jutting out, still firm, but with just the slightest jiggle to them when she walked. The delicate netting of fine lace visible under the sheer blouse lent a soft femininity, and was far sexier than a bra would have been under the see-through blouse. She noted the shaded trace of the dark disks of her aureoles showed through the filmy fabric.

But those damned shorts he insisted on were another thing! They were definitely too small for her, as she told him countless times. She shimmied and struggled mightily to get them up over her hips, and had to suck in her belly to snap them closed. The denim was tightly fitted to the contours of her ass; the little shorts left the entire lengths of her tall legs deliciously bare. When she turned to look over her shoulder, she saw what she feared most: her cheeks were barely confined, and threatened to peek out below with the slightest movement. She flushed with embarrassment at the thought of what she might look like out in the streets with her ass hanging out, and yet she secretly relished the deliciously wicked feelings, getting hot at the very thought of parading around in the seductive outfit. She felt like a whore. The thought thrilled her. And when she gave Decker her appraisal, he smiled broadly and gave her a big kiss, assuring her that that was exactly what she looked like!

Decker lived several blocks from the beach and its modest community boardwalk. And it was there they headed for their stroll, him in a pair of thin running shorts and a sleek spandex jacket, and her in that brazen, sexy outfit, decidedly self-conscious, perched on four-inch heels, walking erect and upright, her cheeks burning, feeling the lecherous glances of the men who stopped to stare, and the envious glares from the women the passed along the crowded streets. Gloria was profoundly grateful for her large dark glasses.

At this time of year, the place was crawling with tourists and even a few residents who couldn't resist the call of the sea on such a brilliant day. But even in a crowd that had more than its fair share of healthy young girls and gorgeous confident women—hard, athletic bodies, tanned and glowing in the sun—even among this stiff competition, the mouthwatering, stately brunette in the scanty outfit created quite a stir, left a trail of men leering in her wake.

Gloria seemed quite naturally to move through a crowd with a certain dignity—that, proud aloof air that had first attracted Decker to her. She looked neither right nor left, ignoring the bold glances, the hungry eyes that devoured her as she walked. And if she was suffering behind those dark glasses, you couldn't tell from her regal bearing. After several blocks, Decker asked solicitously how she was doing, and she whispered a plea to be allowed to go back. He laughed, and gave her an affectionate pat on her denimed behind. But he led her on two more circuits past the little shops and cafes, and the gawking tourists, pausing here and there, before he relented, and they began to wend their way back to his place.

Now back in the cool darkness of his living room Gloria, still flushed and exhilarated from her exhibitionistic outing, sat on the deep pile carpet at his feet. She slipped off her heels, and folded her long legs under her, leaning against his chair, her head rested against the padded arm. Decker reached down, his fingers drawn to her silky hair, which he sampled while they talked. It was then that she managed to bring up the subject of Sarah.

She told him of her fears, her deep misgivings at what they had done. It was reckless, and she was crazy to agree. And now she was frantic with worry about what Sarah might do. Decker waited till she finished, absently toying with her hair, saying not a word.

Then he spoke to her. In a calm reasoned voice, he told her that he agreed with her. It was true that they had begun something with Sarah, and it was also true that it had been left undone. But she must not now apologize to Sarah, or try to explain away what had happened. Instead, she must confront Sarah. Sarah must be brought even closer.

The strength of her refusal came as a mild surprise to Decker. She shook her head vehemently. It was impossible! He was going to far. It was reckless. Dangerous. And she wanted no part of it!

But then he talked to her in that low dreamy voice of his, calm and steady. He argued that if Sarah were drawn even closer, more intimately involved with them, then their secret would also be her secret. It would be much safer that way, he assured her.

It was important that they meet again, he explained. He

was sure that, if approached in the right way, Sarah would consent to another visit. It would have to be done skillfully; he was sure that Gloria would find a way of carrying out the delicate assignment. And so he talked on, steadily wearing down her resistance, until, in the end, she capitulated to that low, velvety voice, even as she knew she would. She allowed herself to be half-convinced that maybe he was right. But right or wrong, she knew she would do what he wanted. She would be held in that implacable will until she submitted, and only then would he release her.

And so, with a sigh of resignation, she had agreed. She would wait for the right opportunity to approach Sarah and offer another invitation. She was to be told that Decker was having some friends over for drinks and hoped she could join them. She could say that he wanted to see her again—but nothing more. The invitation must be simply laid out. Absolutely no pressure, he warned her. Gloria should invite her, and then ask Sarah to think it over for a day or two. It was essential, and this he emphasized, that the young woman make the decision to come freely, of her own accord.

That Monday, Gloria saw Sarah several times, but never alone. But on Tuesday morning she happened to see the slim blonde turn down the hall on her way to the ladies room. Gloria knew that that particular restroom was not much used, and so she hurried down the hall after the girl.

She waited in the outer room, leaning against the sinks, her palms sweating and heart pounding. At the flush of the toilet, she quickly turned to the mirror, pretending to adjust her hair. When Sarah came out, their eyes met. It was an awkward moment, but Gloria handled it with tact, having rehearsed what she intended to say over and over again.

She spoke to her as a friend, woman to woman. She asked how Sarah was doing, her searching eyes filled with kindly solicitude. It was important to personalize their relationship in the first few words, to break through the old roles of boss and subordinate that had been shattered in any case. That meant she must be willing to open herself to greater intimacy, something unimaginable where Sarah was concerned only a few weeks short weeks ago. So much had changed between them. Her tone was sincere, genuinely caring, with just a tinge of embarrassed regret.

She alluded only vaguely to the incident that hung between them, and came close to apologizing, using, she hoped, just the right amount of humility. "Don't apologize!" he had warned her. So instead she asked about Sarah, speaking as a confidant, someone who hoped she had not been too disturbed by what she saw. She knew it must have been upsetting, but really there were some things going on that she didn't understand. Decker also was concerned about her, and he felt that she was due an explanation. He really liked Sarah, wanted to see her again, to set things straight. Then she slid in the proposal that Sarah might come to his place on Friday evening. He planned to have a few friends over, just a small party, quiet evening with friends; they hoped she could come.

Throughout this monologue, the young blonde studied her attractive boss with an odd look, puzzled and yet clearly intrigued. This was a new side to the unapproachable Gloria Brennan. The older woman was obviously worried, very worried, and Sarah suddenly realized with a shock that her boss was afraid of *her*, genuinely concerned at what *she*, Sarah, might do. She found this sudden revelation pleasing, in a perverse sort of way, intrigued to realize she had power over the older woman.

Her first reaction was to mutter some reassurances and

hastily push her way out of there, yet something held her there. She had to admit she wanted to hear what Gloria had to say. She was curious about her boss, and this attractive older man who seemed to do dominate her life. The blonde girl didn't say yes, but she didn't say no, mumbling instead something about thinking it over.

Gloria, wildly relieved that the painful interview was at an end, managed a weak smile and nodded sympathetically. She understood, she said. Abruptly, she turned and left, her knees shaking. She felt like an actress who had just managed to pull off the most difficult role of her career. She had done it! And if the girl refused to come, well, she could report that she had tried. At least, she could tell Decker, she had done her part. She half hoped that Sarah *would* refuse the invitation. For, in her opinion, things had gone quite far enough in this dangerous game. And she would have to tell him so!

CHAPTER TWELVE

GLORIA OPENED THE DOOR wearing the engaging smile of a congenial hostess. Sarah was relieved to see her boss completely dressed his time, in a rather fashionable outfit: a loose sweeping skirt of muted olive drab and a matching tunic, belted at the waist, with a pair of heels that matched her fawn-colored belt. With typical stylish flair, Gloria had turned up the collar on the rakish jacket, and donned a big necklace of chunky ceramic and polished wood cubes. Prominent earrings, each a single large gold disk, hung from her ears.

Gloria seemed genuinely glad that Sarah had come, greeting her warmly, taking the reluctant girl by her hand, giving it a grateful squeeze, and then holding it lightly, as she had ushered her in.

She asked how Sarah how been, in a voice of friendly concern. Casually slipping an arm around Sarah's girlish waist, she hugged her, and then with a loose arm still around her, shepherded the girl through the foyer and down into a large dimly lit living room.

Sarah was uneasy at this sudden display of sisterly affection. Yet there was something comforting about the nearness of this strong, confident woman; even the trace of her familiar jasmine scent seemed warm and reassuring.

It took a moment for her eyes to adjust to the subdued light. A dozen people were scattered around the shadowy room, sitting on the furniture, the floor, the steps, drinking and talking quietly among themselves. Along the far side of the wall a sunken fireplace lent its warmth to the austere, functional furnishings.

Gloria made no attempt to introduce her, but taking her by the arm led her, threading her way through the other guests, toward where Decker, in gray slacks and a black turtleneck sweater, sat sprawled back on the carpeted stairs which curved down to the fireplace. He was engaged in earnest conversation with an intense young girl whose small face and neatly etched features were outlined by the soft glow.

Decker looked up at her approach, instantly sizing her up with those arresting gray eyes. Sarah had dressed in a satiny blouse of soft burgundy. Loosely fitted with billowy sleeves and snug wristbands, its opened collar revealed a small vee of even skin against which glittered several thin gold loops. A tailored skirt of pale beige twill hugged her slim hips and fell straight down, defining her narrow lines.

The girl felt his frank appraisal and blushed uncomfortably. As she stood there, unsure, blinking nervously at Decker from behind her owlish glasses, he muttered something to his companion, then rose to greet her, extending a hand and smiling like she was some long lost friend. She let him take her hand. For a moment he held it lightly, looking straight into her eyes, and Sarah, in her confusion, wondered if he meant to shake her limp hand or kiss it. But he did neither. He merely held it while he welcomed her, his face lighting up. He, too, seemed genuinely pleased to see her. He told her he wanted to talk with her, later perhaps, and then turned her over to Gloria, and went back to the girl he had been talking to. She felt a twinge of disappointment that she had been so readily dismissed.

Gloria offered to get her a drink and stayed with her for a few minutes, before introducing her to a young couple and then slipping away to answer the door, welcoming newcomers while Sarah was left to her own devices.

Nervously, she took a big sip at the glass Gloria had handed her. The drink, some sort of heated punch, hit her like a small bomb, diffusing out through her veins like liquid fire, and leaving her feeling all warm and mellow inside. She decided she should have no more than one of those lethal concoctions. Then she would go.

But Sarah gradually began to relax in the cozy ambience, finding the people there surprisingly accepting of her, a total stranger. They all seemed to know each other. And they acted as though they knew her, treating her as though she were one of them, indeed, as though she had always been part of their group. After a while, she stopped looking for Gloria, content to let herself drift from one group to the next.

She found a seat on a plush gray velvet couch and looked around brightly. In a few minutes, a young man, eager and curious, and very friendly, had taken a set beside her. His name was Alan, an engineer who had once worked for Decker. Sarah was pleased at his obvious interest in her, and a little disappointed when, a few minutes later, a slight, friendly girl came over to snuggle up next to him with easy familiarity. A wide swath of soft russet hair fell in a rakish angle across her brow, while down the sides it fell into smooth even sheets which formed a burnished cowl of shimmering silk around her small face. He introduced her as Nikki; they obviously belonged together.

And so the evening passed, Sarah's one-drink resolution slipped away without a murmur. At some point she found herself standing alone in a corner, watching the passing parade. Most of the crowd were in pairs, she noted. And they were easily, openly affectionate. There was much kissing and touching. Occasionally, a couple would head up the stairs together; she could only guess where they were going. But through it all, her eyes came back to Decker who had not moved from his central place near the fireplace, where he sat as if holding court with the small circle of admirers gathered around him.

She let herself drift over, drawn to him as a moth to a flame. He was deep in some rambling monologue, talking about love, but when he looked up and saw her hovering on the edge, he favored her with a smile, and beckoned her closer, moving to one side to make a place for her.

Now Decker turned all his attention, and his considerable charm, to bear on the young blonde who sat primly on the edge of the step, her knees pressed tightly together. For a moment, he simply stared at her, regarding her gently with his large gray eyes, and when she felt the warmth of his gaze on the side of her face, and turned, bewildered, she was met by his easy disarming smile.

He slipped an arm around her shoulder. Sarah stiffened, instantly alert. Nervously, she looked up for Gloria. The young engineer, Alan, had taken a seat in one of the low-back circular chairs right across from them, and it was there she found Gloria, perched in his lap, her legs crossed, one foot swinging idly. She gave Sarah a benevolent smile and a wink. Nikki, Alan's girlfriend, was nowhere to be seen.

Confused, she glanced at Decker, but he seemed sublimely indifferent to Gloria's dalliance. He slouched back with his arm still loosely around her shoulders. And now he turned to her, and began talking to her in that low soft voice of his, the velvet caress that made her shiver. And even though the others were crowded around, she had the feeling he was speaking to her alone, in an intimate, caring sort of way.

The calm, relaxed tone of his voice was gently reassuring. He was telling her how glad he was that she had come, how pretty she looked tonight. She was really a very lovely girl; Gloria thought so too. She had often told him so.

They had been concerned that she might have been shocked by what she saw the last time. It was, after all, perfectly natural. He knew that some people would overreact. But that was a mistake. One should never turn his back on love, should never reject it when it is offered, for it is the greatest gift one human can offer to another. It must be freely, totally accepted, without reservations, and it must be explored in all its many manifestations. And this led him back to the theme he was talking about with the group. Now, he addressed them once again, turning from her and giving Sarah a few seconds to collect herself.

Someone handed her another drink. Grateful, Sarah took a big gulp, and let the fiery liquid work its magic. She listened to his voice, curious, feeling herself being drawn closer to him, yet afraid of what might be happening. What did he want from her? Where was all this leading? She took a big sip at her glass, and tried to think. Now Decker had lowered his voice, and was purring in a soft, caressing voice, speaking of love and men and women, speaking, once more, as if only to her. She felt herself accepted by him, warmed by his easy confidence, won over by his open, boyish charm.

It was obvious that he wanted her, wanted her in a way that involved Gloria. She felt herself being drawn into something she didn't understand. Did he want to get the two women in bed with him?

She was feeling lightheaded, and she had a hard time thinking. She looked up at Gloria, but met only that sisterly smile, a smile of affirmation, and she felt nothing but love for that woman.

Abruptly, she shook herself. She realized that she had been mesmerized by Decker's syrupy tones, but now she strained to listen more closely to his actual words. His hand lightly cupped her shoulder. He was saying that people should not feel guilty simply because they enjoyed watching others in the act of love. it was really the most natural thing in the world. It was quite normal to find oneself aroused by the sight of two people making love; after all, voyeurism was at the heart of all pornography—all part of the human sexual experience. There were also many people, especially women, he assured her, who found intense pleasure in being watched. And now he leaned even closer to confide to her that their friend Gloria was just such a woman!

Sarah glanced up at the subject of that indiscreet revelation to see that that beneficent smile never wavered; she realized her boss was pleasantly plastered.

By now the room had grown distinctly warmer. The fragrant punch was having its benevolent influence and various couples were becoming more openly amorous. There was an air of barely repressed excitement, an atmosphere of simmering sensuality that permeated the room. Sarah was intensely aware of the air of expectation. She took off her glasses, passing a weak hand over her fevered brow, before resettling them in place.

Now Decker had taken to teasing his paramour, raising his voice to ask her if it wasn't true that she loved to show off what she had, to flaunt it in public. Gloria gave him a sly, sexy grin and shook her head knowingly. Sarah noticed that the young man had Gloria's skirt pushed up and was holding her on his lap with one hand boldly clamped on her nyloned thigh.

"Come on," Decker said to the crowd at large, "maybe if we ask her nice, we can get Gloria to do a dance for us?"

There were claps and hollers and cat-whistles. From somewhere a chant started—"Gloria . . . Gloria . . . Gloria"—a demanding, pagan chant. Someone put a raunchy piece of jazz on the stereo: the loose rattle of snare drums and the more primitive beat of a bass, joined, in time, by a boozy, wailing sax. Two of the men cleared the lucite coffee table and pushed it in the center of the room under the overhead track lights so they would shine directly down on the makeshift stage. By now the incessant chants of "Gloria" had reached a pounding insistence, and Decker beckoned her over.

Slowly, she unwound, swinging her long legs over to one side, lifting each foot in turn, and reaching down to slip off her shoes. Then, with some assistance from Alan, she got to her feet, and stood there a little unsteadily. Decker held out his arms and she came to him. He took her by the hand and helped her up onto the table.

And there she stood for just a moment, her head tilted forward, the light shinning on her lustrous shoulder-length hair. Her eyes were closed and she was swaying slowly to the raw, earthy rhythms. Then, with eyes still closed, her hands went to her belted waist. She undid the buckle and whipped the belt free. Clearly entering into the spirit of the impromptu striptease, she flung the belt out toward her audience, who roared their approval. Curiously, she didn't bother to remove her necklace, but instead her hands went immediately to the top buttons of the tunic, and began working their way methodically down the front of the jacket till she could peel it back and wriggle her shoulders free, stripping off the jacket and letting it fall to the floor with casual disregard.

Sarah sat upright, open-mouthed and scarcely breathing; she watched absolutely entranced by the sight of the stunning brunette moving with easy grace of a big jungle cat, casually shedding her clothes before the hushed, excited audience. She was super-aware that the hand Decker had placed on her shoulder was sliding down her arm and began a slow caress, moving the slippery sleeve up and down her arm in languid circles.

Sarah's eyes took in the long neck and flowing curves of Gloria Brennan's smooth upper chest, the softly rounded shoulders, the upper slopes of her breasts, trimmed with the delicate scalloped lace of the shiny black slip which clung tightly to her torso.

Gloria, writhing and twisting in a bump and grind that was very respectable for an amateur, lowered her long lashes seductively to regard her audience through slitted eyes. She looked out over their heads with unseeing eyes, moving slowly, as though in a trance, surrendering to the slow sensuous music.

Her skirt was next, and once she had undone the side catch and gave it a little assistance, it dropped down her hips and she gave a little wiggle to extricate herself, stepping free of the collapsed pile without missing a beat, to continue her dance clad only in her slip and stockings.

Sarah sat totally mesmerized by the salacious performance unfolding before her, only vaguely aware of Decker's hand on her shoulder, the weight of his hand, the warmth of his hand, the movement of his hand, as it crept along her neck, the fingers rubbing little circles down the front of her neck, edging into her open collar.

Sarah seemed oblivious to all else but the breathtaking sight of Gloria, under the spotlights, alone in pure sensual abandon, enclosed in herself, and proud to let her audience admire her regal form.

Now the audience started clapping, beginning a strong rhythmic applause, and Gloria grabbed two handfuls of her slip, bunching up the black satiny garment, and hauling up the delicate lacy hem to uncover her long tapering legs still clad in dusky nylons. Sarah loved the liquid movements of those strong and shapely legs, dancer's legs that moved with easy grace.

Without pause, Gloria reached down for the hem and gathered up still more of the slippery fabric, hiking the slip up to her waist, crossing her arms and pulling it up and off over her head, all in one sweeping movement.

By now Gloria was totally caught up in her performance. A strange erotic excitement had gripped her. Her initial hesitation, her embarrassed reluctance, had been sloughed off when she stepped up onto the table. And now there was this lusty surge, this wild restlessness that made her want to tear off her clothes, to be free, magnificently free. And when her fine lashes fluttered down, and she escaped into her inner world, savoring those dreamy stirrings of passion, she felt her body move surely, instinctively, undulating in time to the pagan beat.

Now she was swaying in place, writhing sensuously, and stripped down to bra and panties, while the audience roared its approval. Sarah stared, transfixed, her lips parted, her shallow breathing barely audible to Decker who inched just a little closer.

She felt the hand slip down to curve around her delicate breast, and his touch warmed her, and she squeezed her thighs together thrilled by the lusty tingling in her loins.

He leaned forward to bring his lips close to her neatly clipped hair, and the pretty ear it left exposed. And he spoke to her again in that soft caressing tone, the liquid murmurings of a drowsy lover.

He invited her to admire Gloria's stunning good looks, that marvelous shoulder-length hair, her long sensuous body banded in the black bra and panties, those glamorous legs, banded at the tops by the snug wide topbands of her darkened nylons. He told her that Gloria was a very sexy lady, a woman who knew how to experience her full sensuality. And she was beautiful, wasn't she? Men were captivated by her good looks, and women were too. It was perfectly natural to admire feminine beauty. Wouldn't she agree that Gloria was an attractive woman, he asked, edging closer to the tense girl. The hand that was lightly cupping her left breast now closed on her, and she had to stifle a moan. He snuggled closer. Their hips touched and Sarah felt the warmth through the layers of clothing that separated them; she didn't pull back. The hand began to fondle her small breast, slowly and deliciously through the slick layer of her blouse and the underlying brassiere.

"You're enjoying the show, aren't you?" he asked, giving her an affectionate squeeze, "Watching your gorgeous boss do a dance for us, taking her clothes off like one of those topless dancers at a strip club?" He leaned closer to whisper in her ear, his voice laden with husky emotion. Even women find it stimulating to watch a beautiful girl sensuously taking off her clothes, he told her. We are all voyeurs, after all, he explained. Why else would people be fascinated by watching other people fuck?

"You know, I saw you the other day, when you were watching us go at it. It got you all hot and bothered, didn't it? I saw you. You couldn't help it . . . touching yourself, I mean. You couldn't help it, could you?" His breath was hot on the side of her face.

The keyed-up girl kept her eyes locked straight ahead,

taking in the unbelievably erotic dance of the dark-haired woman she knew so well, afraid to turn to face the man who sat beside her, fondling her breast, generating waves of delicious warmth from his firm, sure caress. All the while Decker was closely watching the girl's face. Her breathing had deepened, her small breasts heaving; her blond face seemed flushed. She sat holding her body rigidly upright, her moist lips parted.

"You'd like to touch yourself right now, wouldn't you, Sarah? It makes you hot, just watching Gloria take off her clothes. Go ahead! It's okay! You can do it, touch yourself, go on," he urged softly, taking her left hand, and lifting it by a limp wrist to place it on her right breast.

Sarah kept her eyes riveted on the dancing brunette, let him take her hand, let it be placed there as if she were a rag doll. Decker, his face just inches from hers, held his breath, scarcely daring to breathe. Though she held herself rigidly still, her fingers slid down ever so slightly and then closed over the little mound, squeezing her small brassiered breast through the thin silky blouse.

Decker followed her wide-eyed stare, turning to see Gloria, now seated on the edge of the table, bringing one knee up to roll down one of her stockings, pulling the clingy nylon off her toes and tossing it negligently aside in the direction of her discarded slip. By now Gloria realized the effect she was having on her audience, sensed the power in which she held them. Feeling deliciously wicked she steepled her other leg and skimmed the second nylon down, dispatching it with a nonchalant flip of the wrist. Now down to her pretty black underwear, she straightened up to face her audience in a bold, defiant stance.

The wispy cups of the brassiere, made of a gauzy mesh, did nothing to support, and very little to conceal,

Gloria's full and lovely breasts. The arresting disks of her wide aureoles stood out clearly, the hard nipples poking back against the press of the snug diaphanous film. Fixing her eyes on her hungry audience, she reached up in back to undo the bra strap. With a gesture of charming insouciance, she swept the delicate straps off her shoulders and leaned forward, shrugging off her bra to catch the sagging pouches in her cupped hands, so she could gather up the flimsy scrap and let it fall with blithe indifference.

This time when she straightened, her bare breasts, soft and pendulous, swayed before settling into place with a jiggle—two widely separated mounds crowned with their slightly uptilted, prominent nipples. Now this magnificent woman was splendidly naked but for the sexy pair of sheer black nylon panties slung low across her hips.

Decker heard a long shivering sigh, and his eyes flitted back to the young blonde at his side. Her forehead was sheened with sweat; her cheeks were flushed. Her shallow chest was rising and falling in rapid, ragged heaves. Young Sarah was obviously turned on, hot and bothered, aroused by the steamy striptease. Her hand had quit her breast, but Decker noticed it move in the shadows of her lap as she opened her knees so she could slip it down between her legs, surreptitiously feeling her sex through her skirt and panties, urgently pressing on her needy pussy.

Sarah was shaken by the powerful upwelling of arousal. Her insides seemed to be melting, fusing into a lump with the consistency of oatmeal, the softened mass tumbling and churning with her mounting excitement. In the shadows she could make out the twisting forms of caressing lovers in various stages of undress. The girl named Nikki, her blouse undone, was being pawed by a large burly man. She arched back in his arms, giving herself up to him, her thin chest bowed, the blouse falling open on either side. Sarah noticed the girl wore no bra.

When she turned back to the stripping woman, she became acutely aware of Decker at her side, feeling his breath on the side of her face, and although she kept her eyes fixed on Gloria she sensed his magnetic presence; the power of his restless masculinity, his hunger, so near.

Now that she was down to her last remaining piece of underwear, Gloria seemed impatient to complete the job. Bending forward, she slipped her thumbs into the waistband and skimmed her panties down with dispatch, raising each foot in turn to free herself.

The discarded panties were flung aside to add to the growing pile of lingerie and she straightened up, throwing back her head with an imperious toss of her heavy mane, to stand boldly before them with hands on hips, her head held high. She struck that defiant pose with arms akimbo, as if daring them to look, to admire the lean statuesque form, proudly naked but for the jewelry she still wore, letting their hungry eyes devour her splendid body, the low-slung breasts capped with those audacious nipples, and the brash triangle of her pubic mound rich in its profusion of dark wispy curls.

The captivated audience sat in perfect silence for a moment, and then broke into thunderous applause. Decker's excitement surged at that characteristic toss of the head, and he wanted her, badly. His cock stirred in eager expectation, stifling in the tangle of his underwear; demanding instant release.

He turned to the dazed girl who sat beside him to find her fumbling for her glass and greedily gulping a long drink. Sarah, awash with a jumbled confusion of feelings, sat there stunned, yet terribly excited by the erotic show that Gloria had put on for them. She was hot, burning up with fever, and there was this maddening itch in her crotch. She clenched her thigh muscles and squirmed in her seat with mounting agitation.

She felt Decker's eyes on her face, felt him move even closer, his arm tightening around her shoulder as he tilted her backward. She turned to him and let her head fall back weakly, let herself go limp in his cradling arm, let her mouth fall open receptively, as he leaned over to cover her mouth with his in a long passionate kiss.

And she responded to that kiss with her own, ferociously, greedily seeking his tongue, her tongue battling his in a feverish dance. Then they broke apart and she felt herself being lifted, lightly and easily helped to her feet. She stood there for a moment, swaying, lightheaded and woozy, and then everything went black.

CHAPTER THIRTEEN

A RAY OF SUNLIGHT coming through the window crossed the sleeping girl's face, and she stirred in dreamy response. Sarah was vaguely aware of the luxurious feel of fresh clean sheets against her nude body, and languidly scissored her legs, relishing the delectable feeling.

Instantly alarmed, she shot upright, looking around in frantic confusion. With a shock of clarity she realized her situation—she was sitting up in a strange bed, without a stitch on! Instinctively, she grabbed for the sheet and held it up to her breast. The small bedroom was warm and sunny, sparsely furnished, with two high windows. She sat erect; poised and listening intently. It was perfectly quiet in the house. The clock on the table beside her read 9:45.

Sarah raised a tentative hand to her forehead. She had a slight headache, and there was a woolly taste in her mouth, but otherwise she seemed to be okay. What had happened? It came back to her . . . in pieces: the party, the warm sensuality of that darkened room, Gloria's wanton dance, so incredibly erotic, and the searing sight of her naked body twisting sinuously under the spotlights; after that, Sarah couldn't remember a thing. It all seemed so unreal in the light of morning; it might almost have been a dream. How had she gotten here? She must have passed out. Someone had undressed her and put her to bed. What had she done?

She got out of bed and padded across the thick rug, to the open door of a small alcove, the guest bathroom, she surmised. She used the toilet, washed her face and hands and, studying her face in the mirror, raked her fingers through her short hair. A set of towels had been neatly laid out.

She found her clothes hanging in a closet that was otherwise quite bare, and she quickly dressed. She gave herself a quick once-over in the full-length mirror on the door, straightening her skirt, then stepped into her heels, and creeping toward the door. The hallway was vacant. She saw now that she was on the second floor. She could look down over the banister and see the dining room below, with its double glass doors opening out onto the deck. By leaning over the rail, she could just see the two of them, Decker and Gloria, dressed in their robes, enjoying a leisurely breakfast on the deck.

Her first thought was to avoid them at all costs. Slowly, on tiptoes, she crept down the stairs. She wondered what her chances were of racing down the hallway past the open dining room and making it to the front door. She decided her chances of making her escape without being seen were practically nil. And besides, what could she say to them if she were caught? She would feel awfully foolish.

She decided she was just being silly. Why should she be ashamed to face them? She hadn't really *done* any thing, at least nothing that she could remember. And they had invited her, after all, opened their house to her. These two worldly, sophisticated adults had let her into their private circle, trusting her discretion. She could hardly run out on them like a silly little girl!

Squaring her shoulders and taking a deep breath, she steeled herself and strolled out, as nonchalantly as she could, through the dining room and onto the deck to greet her hosts. The two of them smiled up at her, accepting her like she was one of the family. An extra cup of coffee was poured, and bowls of fruit, rolls, butter, and jam were offered. Sarah realized that she was famished, and ate greedily. The coffee was good; the morning, soft and breezy; the company, easy and familiar.

No one mentioned the previous night until at last, Sarah, feeling a little sheepish, asked how she had ended up in bed. Gloria informed her that she had passed out on them, making some joke about the potent punch. She admitted rather ruefully that she herself had been of little help by that time. It was Decker who had managed to get their guest up to bed. Sarah didn't pursue the subject, preferring not to know how she got undressed.

After awhile Decker drifted off to the house, saying he had some business calls to make, leaving the two of them alone. Neither woman brought up the subject of the previous night and Gloria's solo performance. It was as though it had never happened.

Instead, they spent a pleasant hour or so, chatting and enjoying the warming sunshine. Gloria seemed particularly vibrant and carefree, and Sarah once more warmed to her enthusiasm and easy confidence. When Sarah began to talk of leaving, Gloria implored her to stay. Why not spend the weekend with them here? There was plenty of room. They could enjoy the tennis courts and pool, and it was just a short walk to the beach.

Sarah's weak objections that she hadn't even brought a change of clothes were bushed aside. She really wouldn't need anything dressy, and Gloria had lots of casual things she could borrow. So Sarah let herself be persuaded to stay.

By now the day was getting hotter. The sun felt good. They had moved over to a couple of chaise longues that overlooked the pool. Sarah took off her glasses, kicked off her shoes, and settled back, while Gloria muttered something about getting some sun and sat up to shed her robe. Sarah watched out of the corner of her eye as Gloria dropped the robe to one side and, naked but for a pair of white panties, lay back, giving her body up to the glorious rays of the late morning sun.

Suddenly, almost as an afterthought, she turned to Sarah, raising herself up on one elbow and squinting up at her in the sunlight.

"You must be warm in those things, dear. Why don't you get more comfortable?" she suggested with easy nonchalance. "Go on, don't be shy! No one can see us here. You'll feel better if you got rid of some of those clothes."

Sarah looked nervously toward the house. But Gloria didn't see her pointed glance, as she had already settled back down and now lay with eyes closed, content and perfectly relaxed. Sarah swung her legs down and sat up to remove her blouse.

Through his telescope in the second floor window, Decker watched the young blonde's deft hands as they gradually opened her blouse, undoing each button in turn, and leaving in their wake a widening gap which revealed the smooth girlish chest with her two neat breasts nestled in the filigreed cups of a wispy cream-colored bra.

The sun felt wonderful on Sarah's shoulders. She paused for a moment, glanced over at the relaxed brunette and, with a little shrug, undid the catch at the side of her skirt, opening the zipper and tugging the skirt down over her slight hips, raising her bottom just enough to free the descending skirt. Reaching down, she leaned over and lifted each slim ankle to extricate the fallen skirt. She picked it up, folded it neatly, and placed it on the deck just beside her chair.

Now Decker could fully appreciate the spare lines of the youthful blonde; the shoulders, narrow and fragile with their gentle slope; the delicate traces of the collarbone; the slim breast banded by the minuscule bra; the sweeping lines of her lithe torso; the slight, almost nonexistent hips, tapering down to her straight slender legs still sheathed in the gauzy nylon of her sheer pantyhose. A pair of buff-colored panties were clearly visible through the reinforced crotch of the pantyhose.

The pantyhose were next and once she had worked them down her hips and pulled them free from her thin coltish legs, Sarah felt suddenly loose and just a little wicked sitting outdoors in nothing but her underwear.

Once again, she looked over at her casually bare-breasted companion, who lay inert, half-asleep and perfectly contented. Gloria seemed so indifferent to going around topless. For her, it was all so very natural; it looked awfully inviting. Glancing up at the house to assure herself that they were alone, she reached up in back to undo the catch of the bra and sweep the delicate straps from her shoulders, baring her young breasts to the inviting soft summer breeze, feeling marvelously free.

Decker scrutinized the tiny bra, a narrow band with two curving triangles, delicate, shallow cups, the same buff color as her panties. Watching intently, he saw the sagging cups fall away as the girl nonchalantly scooped up the bra, uncovering the shallow curves of her maidenly breasts, two flattened, slightly raised disks, their faint circular outlines barely perceptible on her nubile chest. The modest mounds might have gone unnoticed were it not for the arresting sight of her perfectly made nipples. Coral-tinted, small and pristine, they neatly defined the precise centers of her nascent titties.

As Sarah settled back and closed her eyes, he watched those shifting tits meld back, all but disappearing into her chest, and then he slowly scanned down her supple torso, studying the sleek plane of her taut belly, and the gently sloping triangle, just where it was crossed with the low-riding waistband of her bikini panties that spanned the shallow indentation between her hipbones. Sarah's panties were of cream-colored nylon, the front panel a V-shaped wedge of opaque satin. Focusing on her crotch Decker was sure he could discern the shadow of blonde pubic hair through the clinging film.

Laying as they were, side by side, the two women invited the inevitable comparisons, and Decker couldn't help swinging the telescope from one to the other, back and forth, between the two feminine forms: The flowing lines of Gloria' long, elegant body, the flattened cones of her gently mounded tits with their uptilted nipples, crinkled now in quiet repose; the dramatic flare of her cradling hips spanned by the low-riding panties, those lovely, tapering legs sprawled carelessly open, fine-muscled, yet softly contoured, shapely as a dancer's. And next to her, Sarah; thin-framed and narrow shouldered, with a her youthful figure and willowy torso; small titties emerging from her flat chest, barely discernable rises save for those delicate little nipples which marked their crests; boyish hips banded by the buff underpants, her thin straight arms and narrow tawny legs parted just a little as they rested on the warm cushions.

Gloria stirred languidly, her pendulous breasts softly swaying as she shifted to lean over to say something to the other girl. He watched the distant pantomime with fascinated curiosity. Gloria reached down for a tube of suntan lotion and very businesslike, began to apply it to her face, her arms, and shoulders, working her way down her chest, her breasts, and her belly, then down the front of her legs. Sarah, propped up on one shoulder, watched her.

When she was finished she offered the tube to Sarah, who briskly applied the lotion, brushing it hurriedly on her front and the tops of her thighs, her eyes averted from Gloria's intense gaze. She tried to return the tube to Gloria, but Gloria said something to her, and then abruptly turned over to offer her back to Sarah. With Gloria laying on her belly, Decker was able to study the subtle curvature of her long, sloping back, the high, firm curves of her tight-cheeked bottom, with the dark crack dimly visible through the tautly stretched nylon.

Sarah, perched on the lower half of Gloria's reclined chair, took up the tube while Gloria shifted to get comfortable, resting her head on her arms, waiting with eyes closed, prepared to give herself up to those small magical hands which already had begun kneading the muscles along the top of her shoulders. Sarah coated her hands thoroughly, rubbed them together, and attacked the warm flesh with all the enthusiasm of a professional masseuse. She used her palms to press into the pliant flesh along the shoulders and then, working her way methodically down, followed a course down either side of the spine. She pressed deeply with the pads of her fingertips, rubbing the smooth back muscles in a deep circular massage, while Gloria let out a deeply satisfied sigh. Sarah noticed that Gloria's lightly even tan was bisected by a narrow strip of white flesh, the ghost of a bra strap, suggesting she didn't always sunbathe topless.

Sarah worked her way lower, covering every inch of the satiny flesh until Gloria's body glowed with an oily sheen. Decker watched those fingers nose down into the shallow dip of the lower back and then ease back up the rising slopes of the nicely rounded buttocks. They edged along the waistband of the panties, while Gloria's lips curled in a pleased smile and she wriggled happily. Then the marvelous hands were at the legbands of the panties, working down the warm smooth flesh at the back of her legs, then tracing back up to sample the silken band of skin at the top of her inner thighs. Gloria couldn't help moving, squirming sensuously, opening her legs just a little more, inviting further exploration by the seeking fingers. But those teasing fingers had already gone, and were now working their way down along the tapering columns of her thighs, to the shallow behind the knee, massaging the taut calves, working down each leg in turn. Once she had coated every inch of flesh, Sarah sat back to admire the job.

When Gloria felt her hands quit her ankles, she pushed herself up, eager to reciprocate. Now the girls changed places, and Sarah rested on folded arms, allowing Decker a view of her lissome back and the small, high-set butt, the pert little cheeks barely contained by the little panties.

Gloria, like Sarah, began her massage on the delicate shoulders, tracing the supple lines. She pressed her palms along the outlined shoulder blades and down the ridges of the clearly articulated backbone, marveling that she could span the girl's narrow waist with her extended hands, both palms pressed against each other where they met on the centerline.

She edged her way lower, her fingertips gliding into the hollow of the lower back and along the upsweeping curve of Sarah's pert buttocks. Gloria eased up the legbands to to uncover the smiling undercurves of those cute little cheeks, which she them traced with a single oily finger.

– 132 –

Decker turned the scope upon Sarah's face and saw a smile of dreamy contentment as she surrendered to the calming influence of that slow, deep massage. When he looked back, he saw that Gloria was now sitting back on her heels. Her heavy breasts dangled temptingly as she leaned over to clasp a sinewy thigh with both oily hands, massaging that tawny leg along the straight narrow lines that smoothly tapered to her trim ankles. She repeated the slow lingering massage on the supple muscles of the other leg, rubbing the scented lotion onto the smooth skin of the girl's calf and caressing the ankle and the slender foot.

Now, pleased with the job she had done, Gloria dismounted and went back to her place, easing down on her belly to let the sun's rays soak in. Decker's hungry gaze took in the lovely sight of the two women laid out side by side, dark-haired and blonde, their nearly naked bodies gleaming with oil, dozing peacefully in the noonday sun.

Gradually, Sarah let herself sink into a kind of torpor, a sleepy lethargy that wasn't quite sleep. She rested with her head on her folded arms, her face turned to one side, and her eyes only half-closed, surreptitiously studying the long clean lines of her nearly nude companion through lowered lashes. And when the drowsy warmth finally overtook her, and she let her heavy eyelids slide shut, long-forgotten images crowded in on her.

Maybe it was delicious feel of the perfect summer's day that reminded her of that long summer's vacation she spent with her girlfriend, Beth. It was between their freshman and sophomore years; a summer when the two girls found themselves at loose ends. The local boys they had known most of their lives now seemed dull and totally boring. Sarah's latest love, Scott, had taken a summer job with his uncle in Atlanta. And Beth, while finding at least two boys at her college to be very promising, seemed a little dispirited now that she was back home. And so, with nothing much else to do, the two girls decided to go about the business of improving their tennis game, tennis being a very popular sport on campus at that time.

Beth was her very best friend—a small, pretty girl with a sunny disposition and a soft helmet of brown, gold-streaked hair that hung straight to her collar, worn with bangs that fell in a soft fringe across her forehead. Sarah thought she looked particularly cute in the oversized sun visor and her fetching white tennis outfit, the one with the abbreviated pleated skirt that left bare her slender legs. Her opinion on this subject was obviously shared by the ogling boys who always seemed to be hanging around the tennis courts whenever they played.

She especially remembered one sweltering day when they had returned from the baking hot courts tired and sweating, and immensely grateful for the cool shadows of the air-conditioned clubhouse. They went straight to the women's locker room, eager to shower and change. The locker room was deserted. Sarah hurriedly peeled off her hot, sticky clothes, and was rummaging through her locker for a towel when she turned to look over her shoulder and saw the evocative image Beth presented when she turned slightly away from Sarah, while bending over to skim down her underpants, her slender, perfectly nude body describing a graceful arc.

Sarah was suddenly struck by the natural beauty of the other girl. Beth was achingly beautiful in her unassuming innocence. Sarah was dumbstruck, her eyes dazzled by the long sinuous curve made by Beth's slim figure, the small, sloping breasts, narrow and pointy, moving liquidly as she straightened up. She watched as Beth daintily raised each foot to step out of the little skirt and discarded panties, and bent down to pick them up. Luckily, the girl didn't look over or she would have caught her friend simply standing there staring at her. Instead, she kept her back turned toward Sarah as she stowed the discarded garments and then rummaged through her locker looking for a towel.

When she turned around again to face Sarah, waiting with a towel held up in front of her, the spell had been broken, and Sarah, still a little shaken, padded off with her friend to the shower room.

As they showered together in the large open bay, Sarah couldn't help sneaking a look at her friend, couldn't help appraising her breasts, comparing the small but perfectly formed pair with her own rather disappointing, flat-chested developments. She continued to steal glimpses of Beth as she briskly lathered up, watching her out of the corner of her eye as she made a few cursory passes over her soapy breasts, and ran a slithering hand down to the hazy half-hidden triangle tucked modestly between her legs. An ache of longing caused her to clamp her thighs on her own soapy hand.

Rattled by her own reaction, Sarah rinsed off quickly and fled out of the showers. She dressed in haste. Her hands trembled a little as she buttoned her blouse in haste, her mind a tumble of confused thoughts. This was not the first time she had seen Beth without her clothes. They had undressed together plenty of times, in that very same locker room. They had shared the showers. And if she thought of Beth that way at all, she thought only of her as a rather pretty girl. Beth's good looks were a certain given, even as Sarah took her own good looks for granted. Yet she had never felt like this! That stab of evocative longing was something new. Was this what boys felt when they looked at a girl like Beth? Was this what it felt like to be . . . a lesbian?

Driving home, she turned the strange thought over in

her mind, examining it with clinical detachment. Then she thought of Scott, and the time, *they* had showered together, in that motel room, just outside San Antonio . . . Scott's hard, wet, naked body under the shower, muscles rippling when he stretched up, the way his swelling cock thickened and stirred when she climbed in the shower with him, . . . and then the two of them, all soapy and rubbing against each other, clutching each other with hungry desperation, clinging tightly to one another, his hardened cock upright, pressed against her belly, while the warm gentle rain of the shower beat down on them. She closed her eyes as a wave of lust welled up in her. The intensity of that memory sent a shiver through her, and she shook herself.

No, she decided, quite rationally, she was not a Lesbian! Still, there was still that evocative image of Beth, burned on her memory, that singular image of pure beauty that would stay with her, to intrude on her thoughts with disturbing frequency.

The two women lay perfectly still, letting the sun work its magic on their healthy, lightly tanned bodies, till at last Gloria began to stir. She stretched languidly, shook herself, got up, and went up to Sarah's chair. Crouching down, she leaned over so as to bring her lips next to the other girl's ear, the swollen tips of her hanging breasts just grazing the oily flesh of Sarah's back. Decker saw her lips move as she whispered something to the drowsy girl. The blonde head nodded and the girl shifted and rolled over listlessly. She got up on one elbow and said something back to Gloria, a quizzical expression on her face. They seemed to be talking it over. Finally, Gloria shook her head slowly from side to side, gave the girl a broad smile and then an encouraging, conspiratorial wink. Abruptly, she stood up, reached down, and slipped off her panties with quick dispatch, beckoning to the young girl, apparently urging her to do likewise. Sarah hesitated for a moment, glanced around nervously, looking up at the house one more time, and then she followed suit, sitting up to modestly ease her underpants down her legs.

Now Gloria extended a hand to her reticent friend and the two of them started off down the back stairs toward the fenced-in pool. Fortunately, Decker was placed high enough so that he could easily see down over the privacy fence that surrounded the pool area.

He followed the naked duo down the steps, enjoying the view from behind, and watched as they entered the water—Gloria plunging in with a reckless headlong dive, her arms straight, her body rigid as an arrow, then swimming like a porpoise, her long graceful body moving underwater with athletic ease; Sarah, easing herself in and standing in the icy water up to her waist, holding herself and shivering, working up her courage to take the plunge. In a moment, she too was splashing about excitedly, wildly exhilarated by the sudden cold shock. The water made her feel alive and tingly. He watched the two girls swim around and splash, cavorting playfully in the water like a couple of spirited teenagers caught skinny-dipping in their parent's pool.

They spent only a short time in the cold, invigorating water before they were hauling themselves out of the pool and running desperately to find something dry. Dripping wet and buck naked, they streaked back toward the house, grabbing clothes and robe on the way, laughing breathlessly as they raced to find the nearest supply of towels.

Decker watched them running up the steps toward him, heard their noisy arrival below, and quickly abandoned his post, to gather up some clothes. He dressed hurriedly so that he could be there to meet them downstairs.

CHAPTER FOURTEEN

MOVING QUICKLY, DECKER pulled on a pair of black jeans, slipped into his sandals and, with his white shirt still open and flapping, rushed down the stairs two at a time. He found them in the living room, giggling and chattering like a couple of schoolgirls. Sarah was ensconced in the big chair. Wrapped in Gloria's large white robe, she was vigorously toweling her boyish crop. She looked moist and dewy-fresh, her cheeks flushed, clearly invigorated from their bracing swim. Without her glasses, she appeared even more youthful and slightly vulnerable, strangely unprotected. She was dabbing her face with a towel.

Gloria had slipped on a black caftan. Loosely draping her long form, the thin robe had a high collar and wide billowy sleeves, and was almost transparent. She padded around the room, a towel wrapped as a turban around her damp hair, animated and alive, and flushed with a rosy glow from the exhilarating swim and the headlong race back to the house. She was busy getting some iced tea when he came in, and now she passed the tall frosty glasses all around.

Decker took his drink and settled in a chair directly across from Sarah. She looked up at him shyly, and gave him a little smile, trying to deflect that steady, questioning gaze of his, the gaze that unhinged her, penetrating her to the very core. As she reached for the glass Gloria offered, the lower half of her robe fell open, uncovering her bare legs all the way up to the crotch. She was thankful she had thought to slip on her panties before donning the robe that Gloria held out to her. Her hostess, she noticed, hadn't bothered to retrieve her underwear.

His eye watched her as Sarah brought the glass to her lips. He stared openly at her slim, girlish legs, following their lengths all the way up to where the belted robe separated at the juncture of her thighs. Sarah's first impulse was to reach down to modestly straighten the robe, but she purposely didn't do that. Instead, she just sat there, perversely determined to give the guy him a good look, feeling bold and sexy, and secretly pleased.

Gloria began to tell him all about their impromptu skinny dipping, but he stopped her, acknowledging with a slight grin, that he knew all about it, having watched them from his window. He made no mention of the telescope. The shocking revelation, made so matter-of-factly, caused Sarah to blush furiously, and she lowered her eyes. She shot an uneasy glance at Gloria. But the dark-haired woman seemed serenely unperturbed. She merely met her friend's anxious eyes with that placid, Mona Lisa smile of hers.

Decker made some pointed comment, mildly taunting Sarah about her obvious discomfort at being caught running around in the buff, and that only increased her sense of acute embarrassment. *Why did he enjoy humiliating her like this?* she wondered. She sat with eyes averted, her cheeks burning hotly, turning in her distress to the older woman. But Gloria only gave her a slight smile and an indifferent shrug.

There was no reason to be shy, and certainly nothing to be ashamed about, Decker continued in his casual, offhanded manner. He reminded Sarah that he had already seen her in her birthday suit, last night, when he had put her to bed. Surely, he continued smoothly, they were all adults here. And besides, Sarah didn't have anything Decker hadn't seen hundreds of time before, he added with a boyish grin.

This kind of talk made Sarah visibly uneasy, yet she just sat there while he persisted, purposely persisted, going on in that soft, polite voice of his, as though he were a kindly teacher explaining things to a pupil. He recalled last night's lascivious performance, a subject that Sarah had politely avoided, asking if she didn't admire Gloria's free, uninhibited manner.

The fact was, Gloria was an exhibitionist, he explained, speaking about the raven-haired beauty as though she wasn't there. The object of this monologue turned to look out a window, but otherwise she made no effort to get up from the table. Decker continued. It had taken her more than 30 years to find this out about herself, but now she knew it turned it on: Showing herself was something she had always secretly longed to do. She got quite a kick out of it. The act, even the thought, of showing herself off, exposing her feminine charms to others, inevitably got her hot. In fact, she got to like taking things off so much, he had to keep an eye on her whenever they went out in public, he joked, smiling benignly at Gloria, who kept her gaze averted.

Sarah could see that the man was clearly enjoying himself by humiliating the woman. Still, Gloria did nothing.

"Look at her, Sarah," he invited. "Isn't she something else? A good-looking woman like that, with an attractive body she just loves showing off? And she thinks you're a very pretty girl too; I know that for a fact." Then, turning to Gloria:

"Watch this." He gave Sarah a wink. "Come here, darling."

Without a word, the stately brunette rose, and avoiding Sarah's wide eyes, she crossed the room to stand before her masterful lover.

"Go on now, let's get this off," he urged softly, fingering the robe she wore.

Gloria studied him for a moment, then, her eyes lost in his, reached down and gathered up handfuls of the loose caftan, stripping her long lean body in one sweeping motion, pulling the voluminous garment over her head and letting it drift to the floor so that she stood before him in all her naked splendor, her head tilted forward, the dark silky mantle partially shielding her face. She stood with eyes downcast, her hands hanging loosely at her sides.

Sarah had seen Gloria stark naked in that incredible wanton dance she had performed, but somehow that had been remote, with Gloria up on the stage. This was different.

It was Gloria's closeness, the sudden electricity in the air. Gone was the playful frolicking of the pool where she had managed to steal many a sidelong glance at that wonderful, athletic body. No longer the easy camaraderie of two girlfriends stretched out together side by side, sunbathing together, comfortable and easy with each other as two sisters at a nudist colony. Then, she had to admit, she had secretly admired the beauty of Gloria's fine body, but that was only natural, no different than admiring a nicely-sculpted vase for its elegant lines. Gloria, on the other hand, seemed to be totally blasé, marvelously indifferent to being nude. When they were by the pool, she had urged the young blonde to drop her drawers, with some remark

– 141 –

about "just us girls," making her feel silly, and prudish if she demurred.

But this! This was decidedly different! The close proximity to Gloria's unclothed body as she stood quietly offering herself for display at the command of this fully clothed man—that was what touched Sarah to the quick, sent a thrill through the girl like an erotic knife through butter; caused her to clench her thighs.

He reached out and took his lover's hand, holding it loosely, looking up at her with adoring eyes.

"Well, isn't she beautiful, Sarah?" he asked in a hushed voice.

The blonde could only nod in dumb agreement.

"Go to Sarah, Darling" he urged softly.

Gloria, who seemed taken to parading around in the nude with the ease of a confirmed nudist, who had been quite happy and relaxed to lay naked in the sun with her young companion, now had suddenly gotten unusually quiet and tense, keyed up in keen anticipation. She knew what he had in mind. Having this mature woman undress in front of her young assistant was debasing and at the same time, wildly exciting. It was, for her, the lethal combination that awoke the unmistakable surge of powerful erotic feelings. She felt herself getting wet between the legs.

But although those powerful randy feelings stirred her now, she let no trace of them show in her expressionless demeanor. Moving in slow motion, like some lovely automaton, she followed his orders, stepping around the table to present herself at loose attention before the younger girl, her face a blank, gaze even, eyes fixed on some distant point.

"Go on, touch her," he whispered, edging his chair closer to Sarah's, inviting her to sample to the beauty that stood before her.

"Feel that silky smooth skin. Go on, she won't mind. You weren't so shy before, when you had the chance to get your hands on her body. You found her attractive then, didn't you? Maybe even wanted her. It's understandable. She's a very sensual, highly attractive woman," he muttered.

The young girl could hardly believe her ears. Stunned, paralyzed with indecision, she found herself captivated by the nearness of the naked woman, who stood only inches away. She was mesmerized by Decker's velvet murmur, saying the things she wanted to deny, but she knew she couldn't. Was he right? Did she want Gloria? She licked her lips nervously, her throat muscles working as she swallowed once, twice.

"Kneel down, Darling."

She heard the words and she obeyed. As they watched the regal beauty lowered herself to her knees, to kneel erect in front of the awestruck blonde.

"Go on," he said to Sarah, "you can touch her." Decker encouraged softly.

Sarah couldn't help herself. She saw her hand reach out, the fingers irresistibly drawn to the soft roundness of a perfectly lovely breast that sat poised just within her reach. Ever so lightly, she let the pads of her fingertips follow the rounded curve, tenderly tracing that alluring contour, while Gloria held herself stiff, and waited with closed eyes, her breathing deepening. The fingers rounded the lush bottom curve and started up the sloping top of Gloria's left breast, continuing on upward over the collarbone and up along the neck, passing under the chin, to finally come to rest barely touching her soft cheek. Gloria moved her head indolently, rubbing against the fingers, like a cat savoring the comfort of a petting hand. A dreamy smile of feline satisfaction curled her lips.

Decker watched fascinated as she nuzzled against the caressing hand, twisting her head to bestow a kiss. Sarah, looking down with affectionate tenderness in her soft blue eyes, drew her fingers across the nibbling lips, and traced the features of that elegant face. The sight of the two attractive females, caught up in one another, fired Decker's passions.

"Come . . . you two, stand up," he urged.

Together they rose and stood gazing at each other, close, but not quite touching. Decker was fascinated by the attraction between them.

"Gloria, take Sarah's robe off."

Obediently, the older woman undid the loose belt and stepped behind the slight blonde, careful not to block Decker's view. She placed her hands on Sarah's shoulders, ducked her head to plant a quick kiss on the side of Sarah's neck. Then she slipped her hands around the girl and into the front of the fluffy robe, to peel it back over her shoulders. Through it all, Sarah stood still as a statue, letting the robe be drawn down her dangling arms, till her willowy body was revealed, naked but for the pair of sheer underpants slung low across her hips.

Decker looked over the simple straight lines of that youthful figure, so lithe and supple, and slowly nodded his approval, sending a secret shiver of pride up the spine of the tense girl. Silently, he beckoned them over to him. Gloria slung an affectionate arm around Sarah's shoulders, and walked her over to where Decker sat waiting, presenting her to him as though she were a proud parent.

Now the girl once more felt the burning power of those searching eyes, eyes that swept her body from her bare feet to the top of her blonde head. She was blushing terribly now, her head tilted forward to avoid his lustful gaze, a demure picture of youthful innocence. His eyes played over the bowed blonde head, the narrow torso and sleek, streamlined flanks, the tawny legs, those diminutive, perfectly made breasts, the smooth skin of her midriff and belly, till his eyes were arrested by the panties still banding her hips. He opened his spread knees and beckoned to her:

"Come closer."

The girl took a step closer.

"Reach up. Hands behind your head," he ordered softly.

The girl took up the mandated pose, reaching up, elongating her svelte torso, the precious nipples riding up, the skin stretching taut over her articulated ribcage. She had her eyes closed, her breath coming in tiny gasps. He saw her curl her lower lip and bite down on it with two small white teeth as she reached for her.

Hooking two fingers in the front of the waistband, he used her panties to pull her hips toward him, as her limber body bowed back in a deep craning arc. With delicate precision, he took the girl's underpants between thumb and forefinger at each hip, and began riding them down, slowly exposing her sex, a narrow triangle marked with just a dusting of pale, blonde pussyfur. He left her panties stretched across her slender thighs at the midpoint, while he examined her intently.

For a long moment he stared at the lightly furred vulva, subjecting her to a minute inspection as the tense girl waited uneasily, her fingers locked behind her head, her eyes tightly shut. The thought of being so frankly, so shamelessly exposed to him sent a wild thrill though her, leaving her tingling with excitement. She sensed a movement, and looked down through narrowed eyes to see him shift even closer, bringing his face so near her pussy that she quivered in anticipation. Decker studied the neat tuck of her cunt, embedded in its delicate cloud of tiny blonde curls. Through pursed lips he blew a stream of air at the top of her cleft, stirring the wispy puff and bringing a sharp intake of breath from the keyed-up female.

Without pause, he leaned over and kissed her there, squarely on the center of that furry little triangle. From far away he heard a stifled moan, short and plaintive. He let his lips linger there, just grazing the tiny pubic hairs while he drank in the pungent, slightly tangy smell of young Sarah's womanhood.

Now he shifted back so he could look up her. He met her eyes and with one extended finger drew a little circle in the air. Without a word, the girl obeyed, turning in place, to provide him with the rear view. Now his eye raked the clean unbroken lines of her lithe back, the smooth, even lines and the gentle dip that rose to those pert, high-set and rather boyish buttocks, Sarah's small, tight-cheeked young bottom. He admired the neat symmetry they presented; the perfect little domes, neatly separated by a tight crack.

"Lovely . . . lovely." He crooned his sincere admiration, his hand drawn irresistibly to that small, enticing butt. With gentle reverence he let the pads of his fingertips trace down over those taut buttocks, caressing the girl's pert, hard-cheeked rump as if it were a finely sculpted statue—contoured alabaster, so delightful to the eye, and pleasing to the touch.

Sarah, her eyes closed dreamily, luxuriated in the warm comforting feel of those firm masculine hands as they cupped her rounded mounds. Without realizing it, she was squirming, writhing sensuously while straining upward, arching back in feline pleasure as those strong, masculine hands held and gently squeezed her saucy little bottom.

CHAPTER FIFTEEN

THE SLIGHTLY BUILT blonde girl held herself rigidly tight, scarcely daring to breathe. Her blonde lashes were clamped shut, and she stood with arms raised and her fingers locked behind her head. She would hold the pose he put her in till he released her. The dull ache in her arms was nothing compared to the exciting tingling feeling, the ripple of randiness that electrified her healthy young body as she offered herself up in such wanton display. She sensed the movement behind her. Decker silently gestured to Gloria, beckoning her over, motioning for her to squat down behind the standing girl.

What happened next sent a piecing thrill right through the girl that penetrated to her very core. It was the electrifying touch of a pair of feminine lips planting a loving kiss on her naked behind, as the older woman, urged on by her eager lover, paid unspoken tribute to young Sarah's perky little butt.

Now Gloria arose behind her, moved up close to the standing girl. She touched her gently on the arm, releasing her from the mandated pose, murmuring in a low, husky voice:

"Come along, Darling."

For Sarah, it all happened as if in a dream. Still hobbled by her half-masted panties, she let herself be led by the arm, over to the gray velvet couch. Once there, she turned to look up at Gloria, somewhat myopically, a curious, soft-ened look in her large, moist eyes. She felt herself eased down onto the couch, her slack body arranged with limp legs lifted up to lay along the couch; head and shoulders propped up on the pillows at one end. The girl felt herself marvelously free when, with one swift gesture, she was relieved of her panties. She looked up in wonder, her big blue eyes widening as Gloria climbed up onto the couch to join her, crawling up on her knees, straddling her hips, rich full breasts swaying beneath her bent torso. Sarah tried to rise up on her elbows, started to say something, but Gloria smiled down on her and, placing a flattened hand on the girl's chest, gently but firmly pushed her back down onto the cushions.

The last shreds of hesitancy melted away as Sarah closed her eyes, letting herself sink into blissful lethargy, prepared to offer up her shallow breasts to the beautiful brunette's tender ministrations.

She felt Gloria close in on her, felt those soft, jellied breasts rub against her own, caught the scent of jasmine, felt the touch of silken hair, the snuggling warmth of the older woman whose restless lips nibbled along neck and cheek, finally seeking her mouth. They came together in an openmouthed kiss of burgeoning arousal, lively tongues dancing, each seeking the other's essence.

Then, Gloria was moving against her, rubbing her tits against her own with mounting urgency, crushing the soft, malleable fleshly mounds beneath her wriggling torso, flattening her breasts against Sarah's modest rises. Writhing in heated urgency, she jammed a leg up between Sarah's churning thighs, to press right up against the grinding blonde pussy. Sarah met the lustful squirming with her own wriggling movements, her arms wrapping around to clasp the older woman in a tight embrace.

Gloria's hands were everywhere, hot and feverish, hungry for her, touching her all over, eagerly sliding over her nubile chest, following the shallow contours of the upper chest, then along the flanks, skimming over slightly raised breasts, lightly grazing the delicate nipples which immediately stiffened under her teasing fingers. Sarah, driven to distraction, gave out a long shivering gasp and bit her lower lip to keep from crying out as Gloria, using both hands, her fingers splayed out, covered her girlish bosom and palmed the soft mounds in a deep circular massage. The sensate nubbins stiffened with excitement, standing up like two pink eraser stubs. And Gloria, quite taken with those small, young breasts, was avidly licking her way over each petite mound, lapping in ever-tightening spirals that closed on the aroused nipples, capturing one then the other, between her teeth, tugging gently on the captive nipple, while Sarah sucked in a ragged breath through tightly clenched teeth.

Sarah squirmed uncontrollably on the couch, while Gloria worked her way lower, licking down the toward the shallow navel, tenderly kissing along the indentations of each jutting hipbone, lapping back and forth across the taut plane of the girl's belly with broad wet strokes, gradually edging along the soft down at the very top of her blonde sex. Sarah was driven wild with expectation to feel the wet trail of her lover's lips edge closer to her womanhood. And when Gloria kissed here there, right between the legs, Sarah whimpered like a hurt puppy.

Now Gloria's growing excitement reached a fevered pitch, and she writhed up along the hard young body beneath her, jamming a hand down between Sarah's thighs to cup her pussy, palming the young girl's cunt, till she had Sarah openly moaning in little cries of ecstasy. With her eyes tightly shut, her features screwed up as though she were in pain, Sarah snapped her head from side to side, making little plaintive sounds that increased in pitch and frequency as her lusty partner worked in a heated rush, determined to bring her off.

Now Gloria switched tactics. Moistening two fingers and spreading apart the blonde's thighs, she used those two joined fingers to rub up and down along the gaping pussy lips, pressing between the slick, rubbery lips to find the sensitive clitoris half-hidden under its fleshy cowl. The surging increase in sexual stimulation drove the healthy young girl berserk, and she strained back, thrusting her hips high up in air, while her partner attacked her with maniacal fury. By now she had the girl gyrating wildly, grunting in short staccato yelps, faster and faster as she raced toward the peak of a powerful orgasm that rose up in her, and she hit that peak with an electrifying shudder, her hips bucking wildly, her straining legs quivering, as she held herself rigid, trembling on the brink. The girl went rigid. The overwhelming flood of rapture overtook her with a high-pitched screech through clenched teeth, and she spasmed mightily as she experienced the ultimate moment of blessed release, and was allowed to slowly collapse back onto the cushions in a sunken heap. Tiny aftershocks ricocheted through her slack body.

Slowly, Gloria dismounted from the warm, sweaty body of her depleted partner. She was wet between the legs, sweating, unbearably hot, shaken by the passionate encounter. Her chest was heaving in long ragged gasps.

She looked to Decker, who was quietly watching them from his seat in the corner, totally enthralled by the power of the highly charged scene of girl/girl love.

Wordlessly, she got up and padded across the room. He stood up to take her in, arms outstretched, and they embraced. Powerfully affected by what he had just witnessed, Decker, sporting a very needy erection that tented the front of his jeans, relished the wonderful feel of Gloria's warm, naked body, still moist and flushed from her lesbian encounter. He sent his fingers digging into her magnificent hair, grabbed a handful, and yanked her head back to save give her a long, hard soul-searing kiss. The naked woman went limp in his arms, melting against him, her arms dangling loosely down at her sides, her warm, nude body fitted to his, pressing urgently against his denim-clad hips. When they broke apart, he kept an arm around her waist, and walked her toward the couch where the depleted blonde lay.

Sarah lay inert, luxuriating in the radiating warmth of the afterglow, coming down from her climax, in a slow gradual descent. Her heart was still pounding, but the only sign of life in the spent form was the rapid rise and fall of her tiny breasts, which gradually evened out into gentle undulations as she recovered her equilibrium.

At last she exhaled deeply, a long shivering sigh released through pursed lips, and her eyes fluttered open to find Decker and Gloria peering down at her. Startled, she started to get up, but Gloria clamped a firm hand on her shoulder, restraining her, smiling down at her as Decker undid his belt and divested himself of his jeans, all the while keeping his eyes on the blonde's.

She watched the man undressing, skimming down his briefs, freeing a prick that was stiffened with lust and itching eager anticipation, felt the gnawing intensity of his powerful masculine need, knew he wanted her. She couldn't take her eyes off his swaying prick that hung heavy and swollen, bobbing before her very eyes, even as he nudged her slack legs apart and knelt between her opened thighs. Languidly, Sarah sunk back on the couch, her diminutive breasts melding back into her supple chest, so that he sighted up her lithe lines he found that narrow streamlined form sprawled in surrender to him, open to his terrible lusty need.

Meanwhile, Gloria had slipped into the chair vacated by Decker. Lighting a cigarette, she settled back, a naked observer, who would watch with interest while her pretty young assistant was fucked by her masterful lover. The very thought sent a shiver of wild excitement through her.

Now she saw Decker slip a hand under the lissome blonde's left leg. Cupping her calf, he lifted the slim leg and moved it aside, resetting the slack limb against the back cushion. Motionless, her eyes closed, Sarah let him arrange her as he liked, limp as a rag doll, content to place herself in his hands. Only her breathing, the rapid heaving of her shallow chest, told of her resurging excitement.

The position, with her legs splayed open, stretched her pinkish labia, spreading the dusky pink furrow nestled in the bulge of her lightly furred vulva. Decker gazed down on those slack young thighs, open in invitation, the moist pink slot wetly gleaming and only inches from his straining prick. His hand moved out to pet her splayed pussy, fingertips teasing through the wispy pale down. As he caressed her outstretched vulva, he got a dreamy hum of contentment from the pleasured girl who had closed her eyes to savor his touch. Slowly, he slid his hand over her mounded vulva, curving it around her sleek contours as it moved up her haunches before crossing over to explore the slight girlish chest with its pretty little nipples.

He grazed the stiffening buds with his fingertips, brushing them to and fro. Then he delicately plucked at each nipple rolling each little stem between thumb and forefinger, tweaking them until they stood up, once more restored to their state of throbbing arousal. And when he had her nipples standing proud, rigid with excitement, he dropped his hands back to her hips, steadying himself while he guided his rock-hard prick toward young Sarah's hot, needy pussy. For one tantalizing moment he hovered on the brink, letting the swollen head of his cock rub up and down the fleshy lips of the gaping entranceway, while the blonde whimpered with growing impatience. Then, opening her nether lips and holding back the fleshy petals with the fingers of one hand, he bore down on her, gradually easing into her tight young body, inch by inch.

The impaled woman threw back her head and let out a long shivering groan as the entire length of Decker's rigid prick slid smoothly up her slick, wet cunt. When he was buried to the hilt, he held himself there, savoring the enfolding heat inner heat of that snug passageway, before beginning his slow withdrawal and then starting to fuck her with measured, deliberate strokes. The blonde gurgled deep in her throat, but except for the few sounds of passion she uttered, she reacted hardly at all. She simply lay there, letting herself be fucked. Perhaps she had not yet fully recovered from her exhausting bout with Gloria, but she was to be given little respite.

Decker planted his flattened palms against her shoulders and pushed, raising up his rigid body and extracting his cock until only the crown remained between her clinging pussy lips. Sarah craned back and whimpered. As he gradually lowered himself he saw her eyes clench shut and she winced at the deep penetration. Now he began fucking her in earnest as the blonde clenched her jaw, baring her teeth, the tendons of her neck standing out as he pounded into her. The feel of silken walls of her tight little cunt was unbelievably exciting, driving Decker wild.

Decker was moving faster now, watching her face, contorted with lines of passion, wincing as each stab jolted her, hearing the uncontrollable grunts she uttered with each thrust. Then there was something else on her part. It started with small movements—her hips twitching. Then she was squirming openly on the velvet couch, as she became increasingly more animated. Soon he was pumping in and out of the girl, while her hips were rocking back to meet his every thrust. He fell hard on her, crushing her warm writhing body beneath him, grinding his chest on small flattened tits, rubbing against the nipples that pressed into his chest like hard little berries, savoring the heavenly feel of that hard young body pressed tightly against his.

By now Decker could no longer hold himself back, and he plunged wholeheartedly ahead, fucking the girl with fiery urgency. Grabbing her by the legs he raised the lower half of her supple body and folded her in half at the waist, rolling her back onto her shoulders so her cunt was up-tilted, as he shifted upward to deepen his penetration. At this sudden shift, the big blue eyes flew open, widening in surprise as his churning cock charted unexplored depths. The girl let out a delighted yelp and locked her failing legs around his loins, capturing the man, squeezing, holding him, drawing him in as she greedily sought even deeper penetration.

Driven to a frenzy of excitement, Decker was pounding into the half-crazed girl with furious determination. He felt her little heels drumming a rapid tattoo on his undulating butt, as she urged him on with lusty animal grunts.

Together they were jogging toward a roaring climax. Decker struggling to hold on for just a little longer, fighting for that last once of control. Then a sharp stab of the most exquisite pleasure thrilled him to the core as the earth-shattering climax broke. He stiffened, his butt clenched

– 154 –

and he threw back his head to cry out as his surging prick started pulsating, erupting in powerful bursts deep in the woman's spasming cunt.

Just then a thundering orgasm overtook Sarah, racking her thin frame from head to toe with a massive convulsive shudder. She arched up, straining to hold him, to cling to the heights of rapture till the last possible moment. Held there, she twisted in ecstatic abandon, crying out as she teetered on the edge. And then, with a long plaintive moan of shivering passion, she slid down the other side, and collapsed gratefully to the couch. She lay there, surrendering to the receding waves of passion, content to be carried along in the blissful aftermath of her second major orgasm of the day. It would not be her last.

She felt Decker dismount; sensed his sudden abandonment. Then a gentle hand fluttered across her forehead, stroking her fevered brow, and when her eyes opened she found herself looking right into the dark eloquent eyes of Gloria Brennan, eyes that searched hers, and smiled at what they found there.

The End

My Secret Life
Anonymous

Over two million copies sold!

Perhaps the most infamous of all underground Victorian erotica, *My Secret Life* is the sexual memoir of a well-to-do gentleman, who began at an early age to keep a diary of his erotic behavior. He continues this record for over forty years, creating in the process a unique social and psychological document. Its complete and detailed description of the hidden side of British and European life in the nineteenth century furnishes materials for the understanding of the Victorian Age that cannot be duplicated in any other source.

The Altar of Venus
Anonymous

Our author, a gentleman of wealth and privilege, is introduced to desire's delights at a tender age, and then and there commits himself to a life-long sensual expedition. As he enters manhood, he progresses from schoolgirls' charms to older women's enticements, especially those of acquaintances' mothers and wives. Later, he moves beyond common London brothels to sophisticated entertainments available only in Paris. Truly, he has become a lord among libertines.

Caning Able
Stan Kent

Caning Able is a modern-day version of the melodramatic tales of Victorian erotica. Full of dastardly villains, regimented discipline, corporal punishment and forbidden sexual liaisons, the novel features the brilliant and beautiful Jasmine, a seemingly helpless heroine who reigns triumphant despite dire peril. By mixing libidinous prose with a changing business world, *Caning Able* gives treasured plots a welcome twist: women who are definitely not the weaker sex.

The Blue Moon Erotic Reader IV

A testimonial to the publication of quality erotica, *The Blue Moon Erotic Reader IV* presents more than twenty romantic and exciting excerpts from selections spanning a variety of periods and themes. This is a historical compilation that combines generous extracts from the finest forbidden books with the most extravagant samplings that the modern erotica imagination has created. The result is a collection that is provocative, entertaining, and perhaps even enlightening. It encompasses memorable scenes of youthful initiations into the mysteries of sex, notorious confessions, and scandalous adventures of the powerful, wealthy, and notable. From the classic erotica of *Wanton Women*, and *The Intimate Memoirs of an Edwardian Dandy* to modern tales like Michael Hemmingson's *The Rooms*, good taste, passion, and an exalted desire are abound, making for a union of sex and sensibility that is available only once in a Blue Moon.

With selections by Don Winslow, Ray Gordon, M. S. Valentine, P. N. Dedeaux, Rupert Mountjoy, Eve Howard, Lisabet Sarai, Michael Hemmingson, and many others.

The Best of the Erotic Reader

"The Erotic Reader series offers an unequaled selection of the hottest scenes drawn from the finest erotic writing." — *Elle*

This historical compilation contains generous extracts from the world's finest forbidden books including excerpts from *Memories of a Young Don Juan*, *My Secret Life*, *Autobiography of a Flea*, *The Romance of Lust*, *The Three Chums*, and many others. They are gathered together here to entertain, and perhaps even enlighten. From secret texts to the scandalous adventures of famous people, from youthful initiations into the mysteries of sex to the most notorious of all confessions, *Best of the Erotic Reader* is a stirring complement to the senses. Containing the most evocative pieces covering several eras of erotic fiction, *Best of the Erotic Reader* collects the most scintillating tales from the seven volumes of *The Erotic Reader*. This comprehensive volume is sure to include delights for any taste and guaranteed to titillate, amuse, and arouse the interests of even the most veteran erotica reader.

Confessions D'Amour
Anne-Marie Villefranche

Confessions D'Amour is the culmination of Villefranche's comically indecent stories about her friends in 1920s' Paris.

Anne-Marie Villefranche invites you to enter an intoxicating world where men and women arrange their love affairs with skill and style. This is a world where illicit encounters are as smooth as a silk stocking, and where sexual secrets are kept in confidence only until a betrayal can be turned to advantage. Here we follow the adventures of Gabrielle de Michoux, the beautiful young widow who contrives to be maintained in luxury by a succession of well-to-do men, Marcel Chalon, ready for any adventure so long as he can go home to Mama afterwards, Armand Budin, who plunges into a passionate love affair with his cousin's estranged wife, Madelein Beauvais, and Yvonne Hiver who is married with two children while still embracing other, younger lovers.

"An erotic tribute to the Paris of yesteryear that will delight modern readers."—*The Observer*

A Maid For All Seasons I, II – Devlin O'Neill

Two Delighful Tales of Romance and Discipline

Lisa is used to her father's old-fashioned discipline, but is it fair that her new employer acts the same way? Mr. Swayne is very handsome very British and very particular about his new maid's work habits But isn't nineteen a bit old to be corrected that way? Still, it's quite a different sensation for Lisa when Mr. Swayne shows his displeasure with her behavior. But Mr. Swayne isn't the only man who likes to turn Lisa over his knee. When she goes to college she finds a new mentor, whose expectations of her are even higher than Mr Swayne's, and who employs very old-fashioned methods to correc Lisa's bad behavior. Whether in a woodshed in Georgia, or a privat club in Chicago, there is always someone there willing and eager to take Lisa in hand and show her the error of her ways.

Color of Pain, Shade of Pleasure
Edited by Cecilia Tan

In these twenty-one tales from two out-of-print classics, *Fetish Fantastic* and *S/M Futures*, some of today's most unflinching erotic fantasists turn their futuristic visions to the extreme underground, transforming the modern fetishes of S/M, bondage, and eroticized power exchange into the templates for new sexual worlds. From the near future of S/M in cyberspace, to a future police state where the real power lies in manipulating authority, these tales are from the edge of both sexual and science fiction.

The Governess
M. S. Valentine

Lovely Miss Hunnicut eagerly embarks upon a career as a governess, hoping to escape the memories of her broken engagement. Little does she know that Crawleigh Manor is far from the respectable household it appears to be. Mr. Crawleigh, in particular, devotes himself to Miss Hunnicut's thorough defiling. Soon the young governess proves herself worthy of the perverse master of the house—though there may be even more depraved powers at work in gloomy Crawleigh Manor . . .

Claire's Uptown Girls
Don Winslow

In this revised and expanded edition, Don Winslow introduces us to Claire's girls, the most exclusive and glamorous escorts in the world. Solicited by upper-class Park Avenue businessmen, Claire's girls have the style, glamour and beauty to charm any man. Graced with super-model beauty, a meticulously crafted look, and a willingness to fulfill any man's most intimate dream, these girls are sure to fulfill any man's most lavish and extravagant fantasy.

The Intimate Memoirs of an Edwardian Dandy I, II, III
Anonymous

This is the sexual coming-of-age of a young Englishman from his youthful days on the countryside to his educational days at Oxford and finally as a sexually adventurous young man in the wild streets of London. Having the free time and money that comes with a privileged upbringing, coupled with a free spirit, our hero indulges every one of his, and our, sexual fantasies. From exotic orgies with country maidens to fanciful escapades with the London elite, the young rake experiences it all. A lusty tale of sexual adventure, *The Intimate Memoirs of an Edwardian Dandy* is a celebration of free spirit and experimentation.

"A treat for the connoisseur of erotic literature."
—*The Guardian*

_____

Jennifer and Nikki
D. M. Perkins

From Manhattan's Fifth Avenue, to the lush island of Tobago, to a mysterious ashram in upstate New York, Jennifer travels with reclusive fashion model Nikki and her seductive half-brother Alain in search of the sexual secrets held by the famous Russian mystic Pere Mitya. To achieve intimacy with this extraordinary family, and get the story she has promised to Jack August, dynamic publisher of *New Man Magazine,* Jennifer must ignore universal taboos and strip away inhibitions she never knew she had.

_____

Confessions of a Left Bank Dominatrix
Gala Fur

Gala Fur introduces the world of French S&M with two collections of stories in one delectable volume. In *Souvenirs of a Left Bank Dominatrix*, stories address topics as varied as: how to recruit a male maidservant, how to turn your partner into a marionette, and how to use a cell phone to humiliate a submissive in a crowded train station. In *Sessions,* Gala offers more description of the life of a dominatrix, detailing the marathon of "Lesbians, bisexuals, submissivies, masochists, paying customers [and] passing playmates" that seek her out for her unique sexual services.

"An intoxicating sexual romp." —*Evergreen Review*

Don Winslow's Victorian Erotica
Don Winslow

The English manor house has long been a place apart; a place of elegant living where, in splendid isolation the gentry could freely indulge their passions for the outdoor sports of riding and hunting. Of course, there were those whose passions ran towards "indoor sports"—lascivious activities enthusiastically, if discreetly, pursued by lusty men and sensual women behind large and imposing stone walls of baronial splendor, where they were safely hidden from prying eyes. These are tales of such licentious decadence from behind the walls of those stately houses of a bygone era.

The Garden of Love
Michael Hemmingson

Three Erotic Thrillers from the Master of the Genre

In The *Comfort of Women*, the oddly passive Nicky Bayless undergoes a sexual re-education at the hands (and not only the hands) of a parade of desperate women who both lead and follow him through an underworld of erotic extremity. The narrator of *The Dress* is troubled by a simple object that may have supernatural properties. "My wife changed when she wore The Dress; she was the Ashley who came to being a few months ago. She was the wife I preferred, and I worried about that. I understood that The Dress was, indeed, an entity all its own, with its own agenda, and it was possessing my wife." In *Drama*, playwright Jonathan falls into an affair with actress Karen after the collapse of his relationship with director Kristine. But Karen's free-fall into debauchery threatens to destroy them both.

The ABZ of Pain and Pleasure
Edited by A. M. LeDeluge

A true alphabet of the unusual, *The ABZ of Pain and Pleasure* offers the reader an understanding of the language of the lash. Beginning with Aida and culminating with Zanetti, this book offers the amateur and adept a broad acquaintance with the heroes and heroines of a unique form of sexual entertainment. The Marquis de Sade is represented here, as are Jean de Berg (author of *The Image*), Pauline Réage (author of *The Story of O* and *Return to the Château*), P. N. Dedeaux (author of *The Tutor* and *The Prefect*), and twenty-two others.

"Frank" and I
Anonymous

The narrator of the story, a wealthy young man, meets a youth one day—the "Frank" of the title—and, taken by his beauty and good manners, invites him to come home with him. One can only imagine his surprise when the young man turns out to be a young woman with beguiling charms.

Hot Sheets
Ray Gordon

Running his own hotel, Mike Hunt struggles to make ends meet. In an attempt to attract more patrons, he turns Room 69 into a state-of-the-art sex chamber. Now all he has to do is wait and watch the money roll in. But nympho waitresses, a sex-crazed chef, and a bartender obsessed with adult videos don't exactly make the ideal hotel staff. And big trouble awaits Mike when his enterprise is infiltrated by an attractive undercover policewoman.

Tea and Spices
Nina Roy

Revolt is seething in the loins of the British colonial settlement of Uttar Pradesh, and in the heart of memsahib Devora Hawthorne who lusts after the dark, sultry Rohan, her husband's trusted servant. While Rohan educates Devora in the intricate social codes that govern the mean-spirited colonial community, he also introduces his eager mistress to a way of loving that exceeds the English imagination. Together, the two explore sexual territories that neither class nor color can control.

Naughty Message
Stanley Carten

Wesley Arthur is a withdrawn computer engineer who finds little excitement in his day-to-day life. That is until the day he comes home from work to discover a lascivious message on his answering machine. Aroused beyond his wildest dreams by the unmentionable acts described, Wesley becomes obsessed with tracking down the woman behind the seductive and mysterious voice. His search takes him through phone sex services, strip clubs and no-tell motels—and finally to his randy reward . . .

The Sleeping Palace
M. Orlando

Another thrilling volume of erotic reveries from the author of *The Architecture of Desire*. Maison Bizarre is the scene of unspeakable erotic cruelty; the Lust Akademie holds captive only the most debauched students of the sensual arts; Baden-Eros is the luxurious retreat of one's most prurient dreams. Once again, M. Orlando uses his flair for exotic detail to explore the nether regions of desire.

"Orlando's writing is an orgasmic and linguistic treat." —*Skin Two*

Venus in Paris
Florentine Vaudrez

When a woman discovers the depths of her own erotic nature, her enthusiasm for the games of love become a threat to her husband. Her older sister defies the conventions of Parisian society by living openly with her lover, a man destined to deceive her. Together, these beautiful sisters tread the path of erotic delight—first in the arms of men, and then in the embraces of their own, more subtle and more constant sex.

The Lawyer
Michael Hemmingson

In this erotic legal thriller, Michael Hemmingson explores sexual perversity within the judicial system. Kelly O'Rourke is an editorial assistant at a large publishing house—she has filed a lawsuit against the conglomerate's best-selling author after a questionable night on a yacht. Kelly isn't quite as innocent as she seems, rather, as her lawyer soon finds out, she has a sordid history of sexual deviance and BDSM, which may not be completely in her past.

Tropic of Lust
Michele de Saint-Exupery

She was the beautiful young wife of a respectable diplomat posted to Bangkok. There the permissive climate encouraged even the most outré sexual fantasy to become reality. Anything was possible for a woman ready to open herself to sexual discovery.

"A tale of sophisticated sensuality [it is] the story of a woman who dares to explore the depths of her own erotic nature."—*Avant Garde*

Folies D'Amour
Anne-Marie Villefranche

From the international best-selling pen of Anne-Marie Villefranche comes another 'improper' novel about the affairs of an intimate circle of friends and lovers. In the stylish Paris of the 1920s, games of love are played with reckless abandon. From the back streets of Montmartre to the opulent hotels on the Rue de Rivoli, the City of Light casts an erotic spell.

———

The Best of Ironwood
Don Winslow

Ostensibly a finishing school for young ladies, Ironwood is actually that singular institution where submissive young beauties are rigorously trained in the many arts of love. For James, our young narrator, Ironwood is a world where discipline knows few boundaries. This collection gathers the very best selections from the Ironwood series and reveals the essence of the Ironwood woman—a consummate blend of sexuality and innocence.

———

The Uninhibited
Ray Gordon

Donna Ryan works in a research laboratory where her boss has developed a new hormone treatment with some astounding and unsuspected side effects. Any woman who comes into contact with the treatment finds her sexual urges so dramatically increased that she loses all her inhibitions. Donna accidentally picks up one of the patches and finds her previously suppressed cravings erupting in an ecstatic orgy of liberated impulses. What ensues is a breakthrough to thrilling dimensions of wild, unrestrained sexuality.

———

Blue Angel Nights
Margarete von Falkensee

This is the delightfully wicked story of an era of infinite possibilities—especially when it comes to eroticism in all its bewitching forms. Among actors and aristocrats, with students and showgirls, in the cafes and salons, and at backstage parties in pleasure boudoirs, *Blue Angel Nights* describes the time when even the most outlandish proposal is likely to find an eager accomplice.

Disciplining Jane
by Jane Eyre

Retaining the threatening and sadistic intent of Charlotte Bronte's *Jane Eyre*, *Disciplining Jane* retells the story with an erotic twist. After enduring constant scrutiny from her cruel adoptive family, young Jane is sent to Lowood, a boarding school where Jane is taught the ways of the rod that render her first in her class.

———

66 Chapters About 33 Women
Michael Hemmingson

An erotic tour de force, *66 Chapters About 33 Women* weaves a complicated web of erotic connections between 33 women and their lovers. Granting each woman 2 vignettes, Hemmingson examines their sexual peccadilloes, and creates a veritable survey course on the possibilities of erotic fiction.

———

The Man of Her Dream
Briony Shilton

Spun from her subconscious's submissive nature, a woman dreams of a man like no other, one who will subject her to pain and pressure, passion and lust. She searches the waking world, combing her personal history and exploring fantasy and fact, until she finds this master. It is he, through an initiation like no other, who takes her to the limits of her submissive nature and on to the extremes of pure sexual joy.

———

S-M: The Last Taboo
Gerald and Caroline Greene

A unique effort to abolish the negative stereotypes that have permeated our perception of sadomasochism. *S-M* illuminates the controversy over the practice as a whole and its place in our culture. The book addresses such topics as: the role of women in sadomasochism; American society and Masochism; the true nature of the Marquis de Sade; spanking in various countries; undinism, more popularly known as "water sports"; and general s-m scenarios. Accompanying the text is a complete appendix of s-m documents, ranging from the steamy works of Baudelaire to Pauline Reage's *Story of O*.

Cybersex
Miranda Reigns

Collected for the first time in one volume is the entirety of Miranda Reigns's *Cyberwebs* trilogy. The trilogy follows Miranda, a young woman who indulges her darkest fantasies by plunging deep into the depths of the online erotic community. But, she soon finds that she cannot separate her online life from her real relationships. Riddled with guilt, Miranda attempts to untangle herself from these relationships, but finds that in the battle between morality and passion, it is the lascivious side of her that always wins.

Depravicus
Anonymous

The Reverend William Entercock is the highly unorthodox priest of Cumsdale Church. As well as running various lucrative undercover commercial enterprises the randy rev also enjoys distinctly worldly relationships with a range of the parish's young ladies, including the nuns. Bishop Simon Holesgood has his suspicions about the vivacious vicar. Joined by a vengeful Mother Superior, the Bishop sets out to get Entercock defrocked. Worse, an attractive young tabloid journalist wants to expose him for the sake of the sensational story that revelation of his excesses will make.

Sacred Exchange
Edited by Lisabet Sarai and S. F. Mayfair

Sacred Exchange is an anthology of original erotic fiction that explores the transcendent, spiritual, or magical aspects of the power exchange in Dominance and Submission. Through stories of ritual, communion, telepathy, devotion, dreams, commitment, and intense personal change, *Sacred Exchange* examines how the bond of trust between dominant and submissive can lead to emotional and spiritual revelations.

The Rooms
Michael Hemmingson

Danielle is the ultimate submissive, begging to do the nastiest, kinkiest acts for a Master. Two men, Alex and Gordon, have sexually enslaved her. They also happen to be her college professors. She opens the darkest regions of her slutty soul to them, revealing rooms of sexual adventure they never knew existed.

The Memoirs of Josephine
Anonymous

19th Century Vienna was a wellspring of culture, society and decadence and home to Josephine Mutzenbacher. One of the most beautiful and sought after libertines of the age, she rose from the streets to become a celebrated courtesan. As a young girl, she learned the secrets of her profession. As mistress to wealthy, powerful men, she used her talents to transform from a slattern to the most wanted woman of the age. This candid, long suppressed memoir is her story.

———

The Pearl
Anonymous

Lewd, bawdy, and sensual, this cult classic is a collection of Victorian erotica that circulated in an underground magazine known as *The Pearl* from July 1879 to December 1880. Now dusted off and totally uncensored, the journal of voluptuous reading that titillated the eminent Victorians is reprinted in its entirety. The eighteen issues of *The Pearl* are packed with short stories, naughty poems, ballads of sexual adventure, letters, limericks, jokes, gossip, and six serialized novels.

———

Mistress of Instruction
Christine Kerr

Mistress of Instruction is a delightfully erotic romp through merry old Victorian England. Gillian, precocious and promiscuous, travels to London where she discovers Crawford House, an exclusive gentlemen's club where young ladies are trained to excel in service. A true prodigy of sensual talents, she is retained to supervise the other girls' initiation into "the life." Her title: Mistress of Instruction.

———

Neptune and Surf
Marilyn Jaye Lewis

A trio of lyrical yet explicit novellas sure to challenge stereotypes about the stylistic range of women's erotica. *Neptune and Surf* is the fruit of the author's conversations with a group of women about their deepest fantasies. What arises is a tantalizing look at women's libidinous desires, exploring their deepest fantasies with a mesmerizing delicacy and frankness. With *Neptune and Surf* Lewis shows why she is one of the premier female voices in erotica.

House of Dreams Book One: Aurochs & Angels
Michael Hemmingson

House of Dreams is Michael Hemmingson's most ambitious work of erotic literature, an epic trilogy of star-crossed love and perilous desire. *Book One: Aurochs & Angels* is the story of Maurice and Kimber, two lovers in the time of sexual revolution and freedom, the 1960s and 70s. Much in the spirit of Henry Miller and those Olympia Press classics, our lovers push the envelope of eros at group orgies in Paris and Hollywood, and revel in the bygone peep-show booths and live sex show days of New York's Times Square.

Dark Star
Michael Perkins

Dark Star explores an underground Californian sex world that ranges across San Francisco's "sacred prostitutes" and pagan play parties to Los Angeles's world of extreme porno video. The plot follows adult video star China Crosley who uses an admiring stalker named Buddy Tate to help her escape a complex Bondage and Discipline marriage to erotic dream entrepreneur Jack Blue. This is a novel of radical sexual relationships that spin passionately out over the edge.

The Intimate Memoir of Dame Jenny Everleigh
Book One: Erotic Adventures
Anonymous

In this first delectable volume of the erotic memoirs of Dame Jenny Everleigh, we find eighteen-year-old Jenny, experiencing her first tastes of the sexual excesses of Victorian England. Wildly curious, and willing to experiment, Jenny finds herself entering a world of unknown sexuality that will dominate her life for years to come.